"Would you just look at that!" cried Mandy gleefully. And there under the bed was one red morocco slipper.

She seized it and jumped up waving it. "The prize is mine," she cried.

"No, mine," said Lord Paul, making a playful attempt to seize it. "It was my idea."

"Wretch! You shall not have it." Mandy jumped on the bed and then fell over laughing, holding the slipper high. He rolled on the bed beside her, pretending to try to get the slipper away from her.

They both suddenly became aware that they were lying very close on Sir John Harrington's bed. "If anyone should see us," laughed Lord Paul, "you would be compromised." He kissed her lightly on the nose and went to the door. "Come along and bring the slipper with you. I agree, you found it."

But I've lost my heart, thought Mandy suddenly, and I don't know how to get it back.

Also by Marion Chesney
Published by Fawcett Books:

MISS DAVENPORT'S CHRISTMAS

Marion Chesney

FAWCETT CREST • NEW YORK

A Fawcett Crest Book
Published by Ballantine Books
Copyright © 1993 by Marion Chesney

Library of Congress Catalog Card Number: 93-90525

ISBN 0-449-22173-3

Manufactured in the United States of America

First Edition: November 1993

Chapter One

IT WAS OFTEN assumed that members of the Regency aristocracy were free spirits, not bound by the rigid moral conventions of the middle class.

But this was certainly not the case in the household of Mr. and Mrs. Davenport, members of the untitled aristocracy. Davenports had fought with Cromwell during the English Civil War against the Cavaliers. Davenports had been outstanding Puritans.

Davenports did not celebrate Christmas.

Christmas to them was still a regrettable pagan festival.

Mr. and Mrs. Davenport had two daughters, Gillian and Amanda. Gillian was twenty, and Amanda, nineteen. They were nicknamed Jilly and Mandy, possibly the only sign of paternal affection towards them that Mr. and Mrs. Davenport had ever shown.

Perhaps if a regiment of soldiers had not encamped near their Yorkshire home, the girls' life would have dragged on in misery under the tyrannical rule of a woman called Abigail Biggs, who was supposed to be their maid but was more of a wardress. Neither of them could remember life without Abigail: Abigail, who had tormented their childhood by devising cruel and ingenious punishments. It might be supposed that the girls would be able to chatter together in private, but Abigail, with the consent of the Davenports, saw to it that they had separate bedrooms and were never alone together.

Until the arrival of the redcoats, Jilly and Mandy were expected to marry suitable Yorkshire gentlemen when their parents got around to choosing husbands for them. But to the Davenports, a regiment of soldiers meant balls and parties and wild officers who might corrupt their girls by their very proximity. The Davenports believed that loose living traveled on the very wind like an infectious disease. This prompted them to decide to travel to London and open up their little-used town house. It was not as if either Jilly or Mandy was to be launched on society; rather they were to be kept away from sin until the regiment in Yorkshire moved on.

A cruel childhood was not an unusual state of affairs during the Regency, when children were always being brutally thrashed for something or other, some sin either real or imagined. The devil was a presence in every young person and had to be periodically thrashed out. Until they arrived in London, neither Jilly nor Mandy had considered their lot a particularly cruel one.

But the Davenports' town house was in a fashionable square, and since Abigail had not thought to forbid the girls to look out of the windows, they could see young misses in flimsy gowns going to parties and balls. For the first time, they began to feel really depressed. Jilly was a willowy redhead with long green eyes and slanting brows. Mandy was small and dark-haired and plump where her sister was slim. But both had been beauties in their way until depression began to take its toll.

And then one day the arrival of visitors lifted their spirits a little. Sir John and Lady Harrington had come to call. Sir John was a cousin of Mr. Davenport's, several times removed. The Harrington ancestors had also been famous Puritans, which was why the Harringtons were now being received. Also, the Harringtons appeared "our kind" to the Davenports, because both Sir John and his lady had heavy colds and were wrapped up in warm, drab clothes and draped with scarves.

Although the Harringtons appeared subdued, Jilly suspected they were kind and was sorry the visit was so brief. Mr. and Mrs. Davenport urged the Harringtons to call again.

They would have been shocked if they could have heard the conversation between the couple afterwards. "I shall never go there again," said Sir John. "Shockingly cold house, and did you mark those poor girls? Hardly a word to say between them, and their little noses red with the cold."

"We could invite them on a visit to Greenbanks," suggested Lady Harrington, Greenbanks being their beloved country home. "We could invite them for Christmas."

"That dreadful couple hate Christmas," said Sir John, and the matter was dropped.

But fate stepped in again into the lives of Jilly and Mandy. A smallpox epidemic descended on London. The Davenports were at their wits' end. Either they kept their daughters in London and exposed them to danger or they took them back to

Yorkshire, where they might be corrupted by the army.

"I have it," said Mr. Davenport, rising from his knees after praying to a God who in his imagination looked remarkably like himself. "Sir John has a place in Gloucestershire in the Cotswolds. He will surely not be remaining in London. We could beg him to take our daughters while we ourselves return to Yorkshire, my dear."

And so the Harringtons, who were summoned, went with great reluctance. Mr. and Mrs. Davenport were slightly taken aback by the appearance of the couple, who had got over their colds and looked extremely fashionable. Sir John's spare figure was clothed in Weston's best tailoring, and his silver hair was cut in a Brutus crop. His plump wife was wearing a modish gown.

They listened to the Davenports' plea to take the girls out of London.

Lady Harrington was about to refuse, to make some excuse, but the sight of the two sad-faced girls with some awful grim maid standing behind them and scowling down at them moved her heart. "We should be delighted to entertain them over Christmas," she said.

"Christmas?" demanded Mrs. Davenport awfully. "I hope you do not celebrate Christmas."

Sir John was about to say wrathfully that Christmas celebrations were the joy of his life, but as he opened his mouth he caught a little pleading look from Jilly's green eyes, and nudging his wife, he said cheerfully, "Wouldn't dream of it. We lead a very quiet life. Never entertain. Hope the young ladies will not be bored. But we are leaving today to visit friends in Banbury. Perhaps the girls may

4

travel as far as Banbury, say, in two days' time, and I will call for them and take them home?"

Privately Jilly and Mandy had each given up hope that the Harringtons would prove to be other than every bit as grim as their parents. In retrospect, Jilly thought she must have imagined that look of sympathy on their faces. Abigail Biggs was seated across from them in the traveling carriage as the streets of London fell behind them. As usual, she read the Bible to them. Conversation was not allowed.

The Davenports always made journeys in short stages, and so it was on the following day that they arrived in Banbury. Rooms had been booked for them at an expensive posting house called the Spread Eagle. But by the time they got there, Abigail Biggs had succumbed to a fever. For once, she was too weak to protest when the coachman, outriders, and grooms said she would need to return to London. Mr. and Mrs. Davenport would never forgive her if either of their daughters caught her complaint. Sir John would be at the posting house in the morning to convey the girls to his home, they had a private dining room, and nothing could happen to them.

So the girls stood in the innyard watching solemnly as Abigail Biggs was at last borne off. As the carriage turned out of the innyard, Abigail let down the glass and hung out of the window, her heavy red face redder than ever with the fever. "Be good," she shouted, "or God will punish you."

And then she was gone. Jilly took her sister's hand in her own, a familiarity Abigail would never have allowed, and said, "Dinner is early here.

Country hours. Come inside, Mandy. Do you know, we have the *same* bedroom for the first time."

"I am a little frightened," confessed Mandy. "I keep expecting Ma or Pa or the servants to pop up and tell us we are doing something wrong."

"We have one evening out of prison. Let's make the most of it," said Jilly.

When they reached their bedchamber, Jilly boldly pulled the bell, and when a waiter answered, she said calmly, "We will not require our private dining room. We wish to dine in the public."

He bowed and went away, but his place was soon taken by the worried landlord. "Now, ladies," he said, "that aunt of yours gave me strict instructions that you were to be kept apart from any company."

Jilly drew herself up to her full height. "That creature is our *maid*, landlord. Our maid! It is what *we* say that matters, and the vulgar creature will leave our employ for her impertinence."

"I . . . I . . . b-beg your pardon, ladies!" exclaimed the landlord. "The lady did not say she was your aunt, so don't be punishing her for that. I assumed—"

"You assume too much," said Jilly. "We will be in the public dining room at four."

"Very good, miss. Certainly, miss."

Jilly stood with her head back and one hand draped across the mantelpiece, but when the landlord had gone and closed the door, she darted across to the bed and fell on her back, laughing. "Oh, that was lovely," she cried. "I am going to be free and independent before Sir John arrives to put us back in fetters tomorrow."

Mandy timidly perched on the end of the bed and

looked at her laughing sister. "What if the landlord tells Sir John, and Sir John tells Pa?"

"We will be beaten or locked up in a cupboard or . . . Oh, Mandy, what does it matter? We have always been beaten and locked in dark cupboards for nothing at all. So what does another punishment matter?"

"Just one evening," said Mandy cautiously. "We cannot go to hell because of one little evening."

"I don't believe in hell at all. So there!" said Jilly.

Mandy looked up at the beamed ceiling as if expecting a bolt of lightning to come through it and strike her sister down.

Jilly swung her legs out of bed. "Let us put on our finest. I want to see people, strange people. I hope the dining room is full of strange people." She swayed across the room, one arm stretched out to the side. "People will gasp and say, 'Who are these *shiners*?' and the whisper will go around, 'The Davenport girls. Those famous beauties.' And two handsome lords will ride to Sir John's and sweep us up and carry us off to Gretna."

Mandy giggled and then put a hand quickly over her mouth as if expecting Abigail to erupt into the room.

There were few visitors to the posting house, for it was midweek, and so when they entered the dining room, there were only two families occupying the long tables. But no sooner had they sat down at the end of one long table, the landlord still hoping to isolate them, than the door of the dining room opened and two gentlemen sauntered in.

At first Jilly did not notice them. She was too busy trying to give her sister courage. Neither she nor Mandy had been allowed to eat anything other than the plainest food, the Davenports not holding with spices or sauces. Even at inns and posting houses, Abigail was sent to the kitchens to make sure the food arrived bland and uncorrupted at the Davenports' table.

"We will just need to eat what is set before us, however rich," Jilly was saying. "We cannot create a fuss in the kitchens." She noticed Mandy's timid look and added, "It is our Christian duty not to make a fuss."

"Oh, in that case . . ." said Mandy weakly.

"And I think we should order champagne," went on Jilly.

"But that is alcohol," squeaked Mandy. " 'Look not upon the wine when it is red,' that's what the Good Book says."

"And so it does," agreed Jilly placidly, "which is why I am not ordering red wine. Champagne is a good antidote against the fever which we may have caught from Abigail. I am only looking after you in her absence, Mandy."

At the other end of the table, studying them with interest, sat Lord Ranger Marden with his friend, Lord Paul Fremont. Both men were in their early thirties, both the younger sons of dukes, both recently retired from the military. Lord Ranger was tall with thick, fair hair and blue eyes, a proud nose, a firm mouth, an athletic figure, and "the best legs in England." Lord Paul was small and neat and dark with a sallow skin and clever black eyes. Both were on their way to stay with an old army friend in Moreton-in-Marsh. Despite a career of wars and battles, they had led carefree lives compared to the Davenport girls. They had drunk hard, played hard, fought hard, and seduced every woman who wanted to be seduced. Both were damned by strict matrons as a pair of reprehensible rakes. But neither of them had ever been guilty of chasing virgins.

"Look at that," drawled Lord Paul. "Did you ever see such bonnets?"

The girls' "finest" consisted of drab mud-colored gowns and coal-scuttle bonnets.

"No maid," commented Lord Ranger, but without much interest in his voice. "No doubt some dragon will join them presently."

But both began to look down the table with increasing interest as champagne was produced. They could not see the faces of the girls, for their bonnets acted like horse blinkers.

Jilly drank one glass of champagne. Then she untied the strings of her bonnet. "You're never going to take your hat off and show your hair," cried Mandy. "Saint Paul said—"

"I am wearing a cap underneath and so are you, and I am too hot," said Jilly. She removed her hat to reveal a plain white muslin cap.

"Well," said Mandy, made bold by champagne, "I may as well do the same. Have you noticed that roaring fire, Jilly? I am so used to being cold."

Soon both bonnets were hanging by their strings from the chairbacks. Lord Ranger put up his quizzing glass. The Davenport girls, despite their age, had not yet been allowed to put their hair up. Jilly's red hair spilled down her back in a glorious shining cascade of color. Amanda's was a riot of dusky curls. Champagne and warmth and freedom from the oppressive presence of Abigail Biggs had restored to them all the beauty they had lost in London.

"They're turning into a pair of beauties before our eyes," remarked Lord Paul. "Let's join 'em."

"We never have anything to do with young misses," said Lord Ranger. "That pair spell trouble. Despite the glory of their hair, their clothes are expensive but very dowdy. There are stern parents in the background, my friend."

And then Lord Ranger found that Jilly was looking full at him. Jilly decided that he was the most wicked-looking man she had ever seen from his mocking blue eyes to his long, long legs, which were stretched out in front of him under the high table. He endured her gaze for a few moments and then quite deliberately winked. Jilly promptly winked back. She felt elated and free and not at all like her usual cowed self.

"Not ladies after all," said Lord Ranger, amused. "I think we *should* join them, Paul."

But the landlord, seeing what they were about to do, stepped in. He explained that the Davenports' coachman had told him to make sure the misses came to no harm, that their parents were very, very strict. Also, their maid had left him a list of instructions. Sir John Harrington was collecting them in the morning. He, the landlord, had allowed them to give up their private parlor and eat in the public dining room and he sincerely hoped Sir John would not be furious with him for allowing them to do so, but the elder Miss Davenport had been very high and mighty about her wishes. Both men, who had half risen from their seats, ruefully sat down again, much to Jilly's relief, for the horrified look on her younger sister's face had sobered her.

Very conscious of the men's eyes on them, they at last left the table, both quite drunk. When they got to their bedroom, Jilly strutted up and down, doing an impersonation of Abigail, and then both laughed till they cried. Then they had a pillow fight, and then they chased each other round the room, rolling on and off the bed and shrieking with delight until angry guests hammered on the walls and called for quiet.

At last they fell asleep, a deep sleep caused by champagne and the first warm room in which they had ever slept in winter.

Jilly was the first to wake. She yawned and picked up her little fob watch, which she had placed on the table beside the bed the night before, and squinted at it. At first she turned it this way and that, unable to believe her eyes. Then she let out a shriek of dismay. Mandy struggled awake, crying, "What is it? Is Abigail back?"

"It is past eleven," said Jilly tremulously, "and Sir John is to call for us at nine. Oh, what if he has left in a fury? Why did no one wake us?"

Both made a scrambled toilet and scampered down the stairs. The landlord glared at them. "Sir John is in the coffee room," he said.

That glare terrified them. Sir John must be furious. But the landlord was in a bad mood because he had tried to make trouble for Jilly, whom he considered far too uppity, and so he had told Sir John about the girls drinking champagne and eating in the public dining room, to which Sir John had said with raised eyebrows, "What on earth has that to do with me? Let the poor little things enjoy their sleep; get me the newspapers and coffee, or are you prepared to stand there all day telling tales?"

Sir John looked up from his newspaper and saw the two dowdy misses in front of him. The elder girl, he noticed, was trying to put a bold front on it, but she held her sister's hand tightly. The younger one gazed on him with wide, scared eyes and said in a trembling voice, "We are so very sorry, Sir John."

He stood up and made them a courtly bow. "I passed a pleasant morning and I am glad you slept well. Have you eaten?"

"No, sir," said Jilly.

"Hey, you must eat, ladies. What would you like?"

"Just a little toast," whispered Mandy.

"And coffee?"

"Chocolate, please," said Jilly, beginning to relax slightly.

He called to a passing waiter and ordered chocolate and toast for both of them. He tried to make conversation, but both girls, by a sort of unspoken communication, had remembered the presence of the waiting Lady Harrington, who would no doubt beat them or lock them in a cupboard or both. So Sir John tactfully picked up his newspaper and continued to read until they were finished.

Neither Mandy nor Jilly really saw much of the countryside on the journey to Greenbanks, Sir John's home. Nor did they appreciate the beauty of Sir John's home when they arrived. Greenbanks was an old house of mellow golden Cotswold stone, so old and long and low and sprawling, it seemed to have settled comfortably into the landscape, rather like the Harringtons themselves.

Sir John ushered them into a long, low drawing room. Lady Harrington rose to meet them. "I have been so worried," she cried. "Why are you come so late?"

"If we are to be locked in a cupboard," said Jilly, "may we please be locked in the same cupboard?"

"What cupboard? What is this?" Lady Harrington's eyes flew to her husband's face.

"They slept late. I did not disturb them," said Sir John. "The fault is mine."

"But why on earth should I put you both in the same cupboard?" exclaimed Lady Harrington. "Is that a new ton word for bedchamber?"

Jilly giggled with relief. "My lady, we are used to being locked in cupboards as punishment."

Husband and wife exchanged shocked glances. Lady Harrington said firmly, "No one punishes anyone here. You are here to enjoy yourselves. Christmas is still a few weeks away, but there are plenty of balls and parties to go to."

The door opened and a lady and gentlemen came in, the lady carrying a chubby baby. "My son, James, and his wife, Betty," said Lady Harrington proudly. "And that is young Master Charles."

It was like opening a box of delights, thought the girls. First there was to be no punishment, then the talk of balls and parties and Christmas, and now this son and daughter who carried around their own baby instead of leaving it in the nursery with the maid. But there was more to come.

"After you have seen your rooms," said Lady Harrington, "we will have a cold collation. Then, James, dear, the village pond is hard frozen and we have plenty of skates. Why do you not take the girls out and give them a spin on the ice?"

"We cannot skate," said Mandy, wide-eyed.

"Then you will learn," said Lady Harrington. "Come, and I will take you to your rooms."

The house was flooded with shafts of sunlight striking through the old mullioned windows. The air smelled of flowers and woodsmoke from the many fires. Lady Harrington led the way up a shallow staircase and along an old passage full of little steps up and steps down. "This is your bedroom, Miss Davenport. Yours is next to it, Miss Amanda."

"Lady Harrington." Jilly took a deep breath. "Would you please call us Jilly and Mandy?"

"Such pretty names. Of course I shall. I shall leave you to wash and change. Ah, there you are, Peg. Peg will fix your hair. She is an excellent lady's maid."

The girls shyly waited while Peg selected gowns for them from the drab selection the housemaids were putting away in the closets. Then Jilly sat down at the toilet table first while Peg brushed down her hair and then began to deftly put it up. Mother would be furious, thought Jilly, but Mother was not here in this wonderland. Next it was Mandy's turn.

When they were finally taken to the dining room, where the Harrington family had been augmented by the presence of the local squire, Sir William Black, his wife, and two noisy children, Jilly and Mandy felt very fashionable and grand and did not notice the compassionate look Lady Harrington gave their gowns or know that that lady was already deciding to hire a dressmaker to alter their clothes.

Jilly and Mandy were bewildered by the easygoing meal, the squire's teasing, the noise of the children, who chased each other round the table and under the table, the barking of several old dogs, and the way in which no one seemed to condemn them for anything at all.

The "scratch" meal, which was how Lady Harrington described it, seemed delicious to them.

Jilly began to wonder whether the offer of skating was to be forgotten, but James finally wiped his mouth on the tablecloth and rose to his feet. "Come along, Jilly and Mandy," he said. "Skating time."

Lord Ranger and Lord Paul had established themselves at their host's mansion a few miles distant from the Harringtons'. They were staying with Colonel Tenby and were delighted to find not only his beautiful niece, Lady Harriet John, in residence, but her equally pretty friend, Lucinda Darcy. That afternoon they decided to ride out before the light failed.

They were approaching the nearby village of Benham St. Anne's when they heard laughter and shrieks. Lord Ranger reined in his horse and pointed with his riding crop. "Over there, Paul. They're skating on the pond. What fun! Let's go and see."

They rode forward and down towards a circular village pond. Lord Ranger immediately recognized the redhead from the inn as both men dismounted and walked to the edge of the pond. Jilly was being led round the ice by James while Mandy watched.

"I am exhausted," they heard James cry. "You misses must try on your own."

An imp of mischief sparkled in Lord Ranger's eyes. "Can we help?" Jilly saw him, gasped, lost her footing, and slid down onto the ice. James helped her up and said to the two men, "I have my hands full."

Lord Ranger and Lord Paul introduced themselves after James had introduced himself and Jilly and Mandy. "We have plenty of skates in the hut over there," said James, "if you wish to help my young ladies find their feet."

"I would not even try," said Jilly. "We are quite hopeless."

"We shall see," was all Lord Ranger would say.

He and Paul tied on skates. Lord Ranger skated up to Jilly. "You cross arms with me like so," he said, "and then try to relax."

She shyly did as she was bid, glancing up at his handsome profile. She stumbled and he caught her round the waist and cried, "Confidence, Miss Davenport." And then all at once, she was skating. She thought afterwards that it must have taken longer than that, but it seemed as if one moment she was floundering and stumbling, and then the next, she was sailing round the ice, held by those strong hands. The sky above sparkled with bright stars, for the sun had long ago disappeared behind the Cotswold hills. White frost glittered on the surrounding trees and grass. Servants had placed lanterns around the pond, which cast a golden light over the black, glassy ice. They changed partners, Mandy with Lord Ranger and Jilly with Lord Paul, but for some reason the girls immediately seemed to lose their footing, and so they changed partners back again.

And then Lord Ranger swung Jilly to a halt. "We must go," he said, "and so must you. Mr. Harrington has come back for you." And there was James signaling from the edge of the pond. The girls had not been aware of his leaving.

"Thank you," said Jilly shyly.

Lord Ranger smiled down at her in a friendly way. "We are neighbors, so we shall meet again." And with those last magic words, he and Lord Paul mounted their horses and rode off.

When the girls reached Jilly's bedroom after being instructed to ring for the maid when they were ready to dress for dinner, Mandy sat down suddenly in front of the fire and burst into tears.

Jilly crouched down beside her. "What is it?" she cried. "What happened? Did Lord Paul insult you?"

She shook her head and smiled through her tears. "He was everything that is kind and charming. It is all too much for me, Jilly, the fun and the laughter and the freedom."

And Jilly held her close and began to cry as well.

Chapter Two

ADY HARRINGTON REFLECTED at dinner that evening that Mrs. Davenport might at least have supplied her daughters with some white muslin gowns, the usual fashion for the young miss. Both were again wearing identical gowns, this time of a dark purple silk, both with very high necklines and no flounces or bows, sleeves long and tight at the wrist. And why dress them the same? They did not look alike. Jilly was tall and slim with that fiery red hair, and Mandy was small and plump and dark-haired. What set them apart from other young ladies was the sheer beauty of their eyes. Jilly's were grass green, fairy green, like shining emeralds, and Mandy's were huge and very blue, like the summer sea. Proper dressing would do miracles for them.

Besides, Lady Harrington had been intrigued to learn from her son about Lord Ranger and Lord Paul. Before dinner, she had sent a boy out to scout around for news. Gossip flowed easily in the countryside, and the boy returned with a short biography of both men, including their parentage and the depressing fact that Colonel Tenby also had charming ladies staying at his home as well.

"So kind of Lord Ranger and Lord Paul to teach

Jilly and Mandy to skate," said Lady Harrington. "The least we can do is to invite them to dinner."

Sir John's eyes sparkled. He knew his wife had started to matchmake. "By all means, my love. I can send the boy over with an invitation this very evening. What about tomorrow night?"

"Too early," said Lady Harrington quickly. The village dressmaker was exceptionally good. Get the woman up here first thing, see what she could do with those dowdy clothes, and then issue the invitation. "I will let you know tomorrow," she said.

Jilly felt quite breathless with excitement. She had not thought to see Lord Ranger again. It had seemed too much to hope for. But if he came, he might sit next to her at the dinner table, he would be in the same room. Mandy thought of Lord Paul with his amused drawling voice and the way his clever eyes teased her. Neither girl had ever thought before of love. Marriage was something worthy that would be arranged for them by their parents. Then, instead of being under the rule of their parents, they would each be under the rule of some man. They had not read romances, had not been allowed to, and yet occasionally rosy little dreams had crept into their minds to make their futures seem even more bleak.

A few miles away, Lord Paul and Lord Ranger were also sitting down to dinner. It was a large house party, so there were twenty of them down the table, the men on one side and the ladies on the other, the colonel being old-fashioned. Looking across the table at the beautiful Lady Harriet seated opposite, Lord Ranger, who knew his host's wife was an American, could only be glad she had not brought American fashions with her and had the ladies dining in another room altogether.

"Enjoy your ride this afternoon, gentlemen?" the colonel asked them.

"Excellent well," drawled Lord Paul. "We had a most amusing diversion with two young ladies."

"Flirting with village misses?" asked Lady Harriet.

"No, we were teaching two pretty ladies how to skate. Their name is Davenport and they are guests of the Harringtons."

"Must ask the Harringtons and their guests over," said Colonel Tenby.

Lady Harriet exchanged a speaking little look with her friend, Lucinda, and muttered, "Not rivals already." She raised her voice. "Tell us about your charmers, Lord Paul."

"Oh, we had met them already, or rather seen them. They were residing at the Spread Eagle in Banbury, and the landlord told us that they were strictly guarded. Very dowdy clothes and the worst bonnets I have ever seen on any females."

"*Worthy* ladies," mocked Lady Harriet. "Just what you need to reform you."

"Lady, *your* beauty is enough to reform the devil," said Lord Ranger, and Lady Harriet flirted expertly with her eyes over her fan, and everyone forgot about the Davenports.

"I do not know what Ma will say." Jilly watched nervously as the dressmaker began to rip up two of their gowns, preparatory to altering them.

It was the following morning. Lady Harrington was supervising the operation. "We will cross that bridge when we come to it," she said airily. "Mrs.

Tibbs here is very skillful with the needle. Are you sure those brown silk things will alter, Mrs. Tibbs?"

"They can be decorated," said Mrs. Tibbs, her head on one side as she considered the wreck of the gowns. "Once the necklines are lowered, the waists raised, Miss Jilly can have green silk shoulder knots and a broad green silk sash, and Miss Mandy, blue. Perhaps your maid, Peg, can help me with the pinning so that we can get both ladies up to the mark at the same time. Then tomorrow I'll get to work on the white muslin."

"So tedious, being pinned," said Lady Harrington. "I know, I shall read to you to pass the time. Peg, fetch me that new novel. Such an amusing title, *Pride and Prejudice*."

Mandy opened her mouth to say that they were not allowed to read novels, but shut it again. There was so much they were doing now that they would never be allowed to do at home, and yet she could see nothing wrong in any of it. Lady Harrington was kindness itself. She pictured the cold, dark rooms of her home in Yorkshire and suppressed an involuntary shiver. How quiet and grim it seemed set against the constant noise and movement and light in the Harringtons' messy, friendly, sprawling home where old dogs were allowed to sleep on the chairs and the baby was adored and passed from one to the other for a cuddle.

The book was produced and Lady Harrington began to read. The girls had never heard anything more wonderful. They twisted and turned obediently under the dressmaker's busy hands and did not notice the time pass. The dressmaker finally said, "I think I can have these ready for this evening, Lady Harrington. It will mean employing a couple of girls. . . ."

Lady Harrington waved a hand. "Do it. I must have two fashionable ladies by this evening. It will do them a world of good."

She stood up to leave. "Could you leave the book behind?" pleaded Mandy.

"Only if you promise *not* to tell me what happens," said Lady Harrington.

No sooner had she left than Jilly picked up the book where she had left off and began to read to Mandy. After nuncheon, they were almost disappointed when James suggested another skating lesson because both were anxious to go on with the story, but then both thought that perhaps by some miracle those two lords might come riding up, and agreed to go and get ready.

But as the sun sank and they began to be able to skate without hanging on to James, there was no sign of any riders coming over the hill.

A cheerful dinner in their newly altered gowns and a noisy game of charades afterwards and the prospect of that book waiting abovestairs quite banished Lord Ranger and Lord Paul from their minds. Their lives were full of warmth and color and affection.

Lady Harrington, looking at their glowing faces, whispered to her husband, "Send an invitation to Lord Paul and Lord Ranger. Two days' time, I think. Their muslins should be ready by then."

"Are you sure about this?" Sir John bent his head close to his wife's so as not to be overheard. "They are such a pair of children. Parental cruelty has kept them very young, and you are planning to throw them before two—from what I gather—very experienced rakes."

"Pooh! I am not planning marriage," lied Lady Harrington. "Doesn't it break your heart to see how humbly grateful they are for every little kindness?"

"You should ask 'em if they can dance. There's a local ball at the White Hart in Moreton next week, but I'll swear they probably don't know a step. Colonel Tenby will no doubt take his guests there, and that means the waltz and the quadrille as well as country dances."

"And ball gowns!" said Lady Harrington in dismay. "I swear they haven't got one between them, and if they have, they're probably sludge-colored and last century's fashions!"

She went to talk to the girls and returned looking downcast. "It is as I feared. They can't dance. No ball gowns. This is war! I will not be defeated. James!"

Her son protested that her young guests would wear him out. First skating lessons and now dancing lessons, but Lady Harrington was adamant. The carpet was rolled back, and she sat down at the pianoforte. Sir John got to work partnering Mandy, and James, Jilly.

It was two in the morning before a dazed Mandy and Jilly rolled into bed. They were to learn that there was no strict timekeeping in the Harrington household as there was at home.

They were to have more pinnings and fittings in the morning and then more dancing lessons in the afternoon. The young curate, said Lady Harrington, was an excellent dancer, as was Mr. Parse, the schoolteacher. They had been invited to call in the early evening to take over the lessons from Sir John and James.

The curate was a shy young man called Mr. Tawst, and the schoolteacher was tall and lank. But they danced with a will while Mrs. James Harrington and Lady Harrington took turns at playing the piano.

When it came to the quadrille, Lady Harrington told them that to really cut a dash, one had to throw in a few entrechats, and to that end she herself had hired a ballet dancer in London to teach her. To Jilly's amusement and Mandy's shock, Lady Harrington picked up her skirts so that all could see her ankles and demonstrated how to perform entrechats, laughing when they all tumbled over trying to copy her and said it was surely harder than teaching them to skate.

Again it was two in the morning before the girls finally rolled into bed. The only thing to give Jilly any feeling of unease before she fell asleep was the fact that the days seemed to be rushing past. Time had speeded up like a runaway horse. At home, time crawled, punctuated by the monotonous ticktock of the many clocks that Mr. and Mrs. Davenport liked to collect.

The girls were to learn that a dinner party at the Harringtons' was quite an event. The house and table had to be decorated and everybody helped, James bringing in branches that still had red and gold leaves on them to be dipped in glycerine in the still room to preserve them, and Sir John cutting fine blooms for the table and drawing room in the hothouses at the end of the garden.

Jilly and Mandy went down to the kitchens with

Lady Harrington and looked around with interest. They had never been allowed to visit the kitchens at home in case they might be spoiled by the servants and given sweetmeats. But Lady Harrington believed that any lady worth her salt should be able to do anything her servants could do, and do it better. And so the girls were taught how to make jam tartlets to give them a feeling of being part of the preparations. They enjoyed the warm, spice-scented kitchen, where great hams and sides of salt beef hung from the beams along with bunches of dried herbs. Lady Harrington looked at their absorbed and happy faces as they rolled out pastry and was glad she had burned that dreadful letter.

The letter had arrived addressed to the girls by the morning post, and Lady Harrington had immediately recognized the Davenport seal. Ignoring a horrified exclamation from Sir John and his cry of "You are never going to read their post!" she scanned the crossed page; that is, Mrs. Davenport had written across the page in her spidery writing and then, to save paper, had turned the sheet sideways and written across it.

"As I thought," said Lady Harrington. "Moralizing and more moralizing. Read your Bible, say your prayers, get to bed at ten, ignore all Christmas festivities, a pagan festival. . . . What a jaw-me-dead. The only good news is that they are off to Yorkshire and they have taken that terrible maid with them; although she is recovering from the fever, she is still weak. Good, we can be comfortable." And with that, Lady Harrington had thrown the letter on the fire.

"No, I have no intention of letting them see such

stuff," she said as her husband protested. "Too utterly depressing for words."

But remembering that letter, she asked Jilly and Mandy, "Have you written to your parents?"

Mandy colored up and looked guilty. "We do not seem to have had time. I think we should do that as soon as possible."

"I would not distress your parents with tales of skating and dancing and things like that," said Lady Harrington airily. "They might get the wrong idea and come and take you away."

"We will tell them nothing to distress them," said Jilly firmly.

"Good," said Lady Harrington, "and if you write it on the morrow, I will send it express so that it will be waiting for them in Yorkshire when they arrive. If it is not impertinent of me to ask such a thing, I should like to see what you have written."

"Gladly," said Jilly, who felt that there was no need at all to have secrets from such as Lady Harrington.

They then helped arrange the dining table with the best silver and glass, and Lady Harrington taught them how to make wreaths of evergreens woven with fresh flowers to decorate the table.

Again another day flew past towards evening, and it came as a shock when the dressing bell sounded.

"You don't think the Harringtons are trying to matchmake for those two dowds," said Lord Ranger as they drove towards Greenbanks.

"You are too hard," remarked Lord Paul. "I thought they looked vastly pretty in the inn dining room when they took off those dreadful bonnets.

Have you formed a tendre for Lady Harriet? She is very elegant but no substance, I think."

"When did you ever demand substance in a woman, Paul? You always demanded that they be decorative and nothing more, and the fair Harriet and her friend, Lucinda, answer that description."

"There is a sort of calm assumption at Colonel Tenby's that we should propose to them, or haven't you noticed?"

"When there are two bachelors anywhere in England at a house party, then it is always assumed that they will propose to two single females before the end of the visit. It is all part of the game."

"You might get trapped this time, Ranger. I sense that under Lady Harriet's soft exterior lies a soul of pure steel."

He laughed. "I might like to be trapped. Here we are. Brace yourself for a very dull and correct evening."

When both men entered the drawing room, they felt themselves being enfolded in warmth and welcome. The air was scented with hothouse blooms, an apple wood fire roared in the chimney, James, his wife, Betty, and their baby sat on a sofa with two mangy old dogs snoring companionably at their feet.

Sir John went to meet them. "Welcome," he cried. "My wife will join us presently. She has gone to fetch the young ladies. How goes Colonel Tenby? Well, I trust."

"Very well," said Lord Ranger.

Then the door of the drawing room opened and both he and Paul turned round.

Jilly and Mandy entered the room. They both

wore simple muslin gowns but of a different pattern. Jilly's had a green sprig, and Mandy's, a blue. Their hair had been dressed in different and elaborate styles. Their large eyes were shining with excitement. They looked very modish apart from that expression in their eyes. The Davenport girls did not know that it was fashionable to look bored.

Jilly privately felt a little overawed. Lord Ranger looked so very tall and exquisite in his faultless evening clothes, as did Lord Paul.

"Now we are all here, we will sit down to dinner immediately," said Sir John. He led the way to the drawing room, holding his wife's hand. James followed with his wife after giving the baby to a maid. Lord Ranger held out his arm to Jilly, who did not know that one put the tips of one's fingers on it and linked her own arm with his.

Jilly had been delighted to learn earlier that she was to sit beside Lord Ranger at the dining table, but now she began to feel gauche and nervous. She wondered if her gown, which had looked so modish and fashionable abovestairs, was grand enough, and then chided herself for such an ungrateful and vain thought. "Are you enjoying your visit?" Lord Ranger asked politely.

"Oh, so very much," she said. "We have been reading and dancing and skating and going to bed so very late."

"How late, Miss Davenport?"

"Two in the morning."

"In London five or six is the usual time. Have you not had a Season?"

"No, my lord."

"Why?"

Too nervous to do other than tell the truth, Jilly

28

said, "My parents prefer that suitable husbands are chosen for us in Yorkshire."

"But you should have some fun first." His eyes teased her. "Marriage can be a grim business."

"So I believe," she said, sadness clouding those green eyes.

He was immediately sorry for having teased her and said quickly, "But you are enjoying yourself here?"

"So very much. But the days go past so very quickly. In Yorkshire one week can sometimes feel like a year, particularly in winter."

"Do you celebrate Christmas in the good old-fashioned way in Yorkshire?"

"We do not celebrate Christmas at all, my lord."

"Why is that?"

"My parents consider it a pagan festival."

He reflected that the Davenport parents must indeed be a pair of antidotes. "I am sure you will celebrate Christmas here," he said. "And there is a local ball at Moreton-in-Marsh next week. Do you attend?"

She gave an endearing gurgle of laughter. "We *must* go. Lady Harrington and the family have been to such trouble to teach Mandy and me to dance. You never saw anything like it, my lord. Poor Sir John and James were so exhausted that the curate and the schoolmaster had to be brought in to take over the tuition. And then Lady Harrington tried to show us how to perform entrechats, which she assured us were the height of ton, but we all kept falling over in a heap."

"Had you never danced before?" he asked curiously.

"No, never. My parents would not approve, but

this is a once-in-a-lifetime visit, and Mandy and I will have memories, don't you see, for the dark days ahead."

"You are very young and quite beautiful, Miss Davenport. You should not have gloomy thoughts."

"How kind of you to say so, my lord," said Jilly. "But red hair is a sad defect." Again that gurgle of laughter. "Poor Ma. She shaved my head several times hoping it would grow in another color, but she said it just seemed to get redder and redder."

"It is like a flame," he said, and sheer happiness began to bubble up inside Jilly. It was dampened a little by the quick reflection that compliments probably came easily to him.

"And what of you yourself, my lord?" she asked.

"What am I doing now, what do I intend to do with my life, or do you want to know all about me?"

"If you tell me all about yourself," said Jilly earnestly, "it will pass the time and Lady Harrington will think I am a success, but the sad fact is, I am not in the way of conducting elegant conversation."

He laughed. "Eat your food and I will try to give you a summary of my life. I left school at sixteen and went into the army. I fought in the Peninsular Wars, as did Lord Paul, and then at Waterloo last year. Paul and I have just sold out. We are both going to settle down and become respectable gentlemen."

"Are you going to get married?" Jilly asked, and then blushed.

"Possibly. I always thought of living in Town." He looked around. "But a snug little place like this has its merits."

"A house with twelve bedrooms is hardly a little place, my lord."

His eyes teased her again. "But think of all the rooms I will need for all the children I would expect my wife to have."

James, on the other side of Jilly, saw that blush and remembered his mother's instruction to look after Jilly and promptly drew her attention to himself.

Lady Harrington had forgotten that two young ladies with such a Puritan upbringing would not be accustomed to wine. Jilly had been too busy talking to Lord Ranger to drink much, but Mandy had been emptying her glass steadily, until Lord Paul, seeing that her eyes were becoming rather unfocused, leaned back in his chair and asked a maid to bring lemonade. The Harringtons only employed female servants indoors.

"Lemonade, Lord Paul?" queried Sir John.

"I like lemonade," replied Lord Paul firmly.

"Thank you," whispered Mandy when a glass had been put in front of her. "I am unaccustomed to wine and it makes me feel dizzy."

"I, too," he lied, being able to sink six bottles a day. "We will drink nothing but lemonade for the rest of the evening and then we will feel well again. Now you must eat. You have barely touched your food."

Like an obedient child, she picked up her knife and fork. She badly needed someone to look after her, thought Lord Paul, who, like Lord Ranger, had been startled by revelations of the girls' strict upbringing.

At the end of the meal, after the covers had been removed and the wine passed round, or in the case of Lord Paul and Mandy, more iced lemonade, both guests waited for Lady Harrington to rise and lead

31

the ladies from the room. But Lady Harrington stayed where she was, and it was Sir John who finally suggested that they all move back to the drawing room.

Lord Ranger exchanged a rueful glance with Lord Paul when Sir John, once they were in the drawing room, immediately suggested they play a game. "Let us play Hunt the Slipper," he said. "I have hidden one of my best morroco slippers somewhere in the house. Whoever finds it gets a prize. I suggest you hunt in pairs. I cannot join in because, of course, I know where the slipper is. Lord Ranger, you go with Jilly, and Lord Paul with Mandy. Betty, you had better stay by the fire." For Betty had taken charge of the baby again. "My wife and James will make up the other pair. Now, off you go."

"We should have thought of some excuse and left right after dinner," muttered Lord Paul.

But the Davenport girls seemed to find nothing unfashionable in such a simple game. Lord Ranger and Jilly began to search in the corridors, in the bedrooms, and on the landings, without success. Jilly was so caught up in the game, so determined to find that slipper, that Lord Ranger began to find her enthusiasm infectious.

He stopped outside a cupboard under the stairs and opened the door. "Perhaps it is in here." A spirit of mischief overtook him and he seized Jilly by the hand, dragged her in, and shut the door.

"Let me out," said Jilly in an urgent whisper, and to his amazement, he heard stark fear in her voice. He promptly opened the door and led her out. She was white and shaking.

"Miss Davenport," he said stiffly, "I was merely being playful. I had no intention of—"

"It is my fault," said Jilly weakly. "I am so used to being shut in cupboards as a punishment that . . . that . . . I panicked."

"My dear, how old are you?"

"Twenty."

"Surely you are not still punished so?"

She nodded her head.

He suddenly wanted to say something really nasty about her parents, but good manners stopped him. Instead he took her hand in his and said gently, "Let us not think of bad things. Where have we not tried to look for that wretched slipper?"

"The kitchens!" she cried.

They went down the back stairs together and into the warmth of the kitchens. The staff had retired for the night, leaving a tray ready with chicken sandwiches under a cloth.

Lord Ranger lit a candle by thrusting it through the bars of the grate. He set it in a flat stick on the table and looked around. "Now where?" he asked.

"Up there perhaps," said Jilly, "among the bunches of herbs."

He climbed up on a chair. "What a hard task-master you are."

"Let me look as well," cried Jilly.

"You are not quite tall enough to stand on a chair, sweeting."

"Then I shall stand on the table," she said, climbing up on it.

"What a hoyden you are." They searched diligently among the bushes of sweet herbs.

"I am tired of this," he said at last. "Look, there are some jam tarts over there and a jug of coffee on the stove. Let us have a little picnic down here and leave the others to the search."

He climbed down from the chair and lifted her down from the table. For one brief moment, her light body was pressed against him, for a second those glorious green eyes flashed darker with some emotion, and then she had turned away from him and was saying in a rapid voice, "If you can find some cups, my lord, I will fetch the tarts. I . . . I baked them myself. It is the first time I have ever been allowed in a kitchen."

"Poor Miss Davenport. Kitchens are the best part of the house. Let your little sister find that slipper and let us be comfortable."

Mandy and Lord Paul stood in the corridor upstairs. "I do not know where else we can look," said Mandy. "Surely we have looked everywhere. Perhaps Lady Harrington has found it. After all, she must know how Sir John thinks."

He smiled at her. "Let us consider the character of Sir John, easygoing and perhaps lazy. I cannot think of him putting it anywhere too difficult, and that, I think, has been our problem. He has probably put it somewhere very simple."

"Such as?" Mandy's eyes were very wide and dark.

"Now, where would you expect to find slippers?"

She frowned. "Under the bed, I suppose."

"That's it. And do you know where I think we will find it? With its fellow under Sir John Harrington's bed!"

Unself-consciously she seized his hand and began to drag him along the corridor while he followed, laughing. They opened the door of Sir John's bedroom, and Mandy promptly dropped to her knees. Lord Paul crouched down beside her.

"Would you just look at that!" cried Mandy gleefully. And there under the bed was one red morocco slipper.

She seized it and jumped up, waving it. "The prize is mine," she cried.

"No, mine," said Lord Paul, making a playful attempt to seize it. "It was my idea."

"Wretch! You shall not have it." Mandy jumped on the bed and then fell over laughing, holding the slipper high. He rolled on the bed beside her, pretending to try to get the slipper away from her.

They suddenly both became aware at the same time that they were lying very close on Sir John Harrington's bed. "If anyone should see us," laughed Lord Paul, "you would be compromised." He kissed her lightly on the nose and went to the door. "Come along, and bring the slipper with you. I agree, you found it."

But I've lost my heart, thought Mandy suddenly, and I don't know how to get it back.

The prize was a large bottle of scent, the first Mandy had ever had. "What would you have done if one of the gentlemen had won?" she asked.

But Sir John would only look mysterious. He did not want to spoil her fun by telling her that gentlemen usually allowed the ladies to collect the prize. "We must tell Jilly it has been found. Where is she?" asked Mandy, looking around.

"The fun is to leave the poor losers to search for a little longer," said Lady Harrington, who had no intention of separating Lord Ranger and Jilly one moment sooner than necessary.

Betty, who had put her precious baby to bed, offered to play some tunes on the piano. Sir John and Lady Harrington began to sing duets, with more enthusiasm than good voice. Lord Paul, after joining in several of the numbers, began to feel uneasy. Lord Ranger was away far too long. He hoped his friend was remembering he was dealing with a highly respectable virgin.

"Do you know what I would really like to do when this visit is over?" confided Jilly, inelegantly licking jam tart crumbs from her fingers.

"No, what?" asked Lord Ranger, his eyes dancing.

"I would like to take Mandy and run away, far away, to somewhere sunny and never go home again."

"Have you no money of your own?" he asked.

"I do not know. I believe my Aunt Margaret left me money in her will, but such matters are never discussed with us. I could find work. Perhaps if Mandy and I could become maids in a household such as this, it would not be so very hard. The Harringtons are most kind to their servants."

"The Harringtons are highly unusual. Has it not struck you that they are very unconventional? They do not have any indoor menservants and have a free manner I have not met in any household before. Besides, I have never been to a dinner party before where the servants were allowed to go off duty before the guests had left."

"They have already done so much for us," said Jilly. "I do not know how we can ever repay them. Do you like my gown, my lord?"

"Very fine."

"Lady Harrington had the muslin gowns made for us, just for this evening, and she has ordered the dressmaker to alter our gowns." A shadow crossed her eyes. "I do not know what Ma will say when she sees the result, but I do know she will be very angry."

"It is always possible to stand up to people. You must make yourself feel brave inside as well as out," said Lord Ranger. "You must say very firmly, 'I like my gowns, and do not dare punish me.'"

"All very fine if one is an independent gentleman of independent means," said Jilly. "Did I really eat all those tartlets or did you have some?"

"I had some, I assure you. Do you not think we should make more coffee as we have drunk all that was in that jug?"

"Then we can take it upstairs with those sandwiches." Jilly got to her feet. "Now I must fill the kettle. How helpless I feel. I do not know where the pump is."

"Allow me. There is usually a pump in the scullery." He poked the kitchen fire into a blaze, went out, and returned a little time later with the kettle, which he hooked onto the idleback and swung over the flames. "I could hear the wind rising outside," he said. "Perhaps we shall have snow."

Those odd green eyes grew dreamy. "There is a hill above the pond," said Jilly. "Do you think the Harringtons have a sleigh? One could sledge down that hill and straight across the ice. Once when I was out walking with Abigail, our maid, I saw some boys sledging down a hill. They were so merry and it looked such fun."

He took her hand in his. "I promise you, Miss

Jilly, that if it snows, I will find a sledge and bring it over."

Jilly laughed and clapped her hands. "Then it must snow. I must see *now*."

She ran to the door and opened it and went through the scullery and tugged the outside door open. She ran out into the night, the thin white muslin of her gown fluttering in the darkness, and stared up at the heavens. He came and stood beside her. The wind rushed about them. "Come inside," he said. "You will catch your death of cold. Besides, it is so black, you cannot see anything."

"What was that?" whispered Jilly, feeling something soft brush her cheek. "I am sure that was a snowflake."

He took off his coat and put it about her shoulders. "I'll see if I can find a lantern."

Jilly stood after he had gone, holding his coat tightly about her shoulders, gazing ever upwards. Then he came out and stood next to her again and held up the lantern.

"Look! Oh, look!" said Jilly. In the circle of light thrown by the lantern, which Lord Ranger held high, could be seen delicate snowflakes, fluttering down.

"Then you shall have your sledging party. But we must go indoors. The others will be wondering what has become of us."

They returned to the kitchen, where, suddenly shy of him, she took off his coat and handed it to him. He put it on and then made a jug of coffee and put it on the tray with the sandwiches. They added milk and sugar to the load and then he carried it upstairs, with Jilly following.

Lord Paul studied his friend's face as Lord Ranger put down the tray and explained they had ended up having a private party in the kitchens. "And we are to go sledging with Lord Ranger tomorrow," cried Jilly. "Oh, please say yes, Lady Harrington."

"How can you sledge with no snow?" asked Lady Harrington.

"But it has begun to snow," said Jilly.

"In that case," said Lord Paul quietly, "we had best make tracks for Colonel Tenby's while we still can."

"Stay the night," invited Sir John.

"We cannot go sledging in our evening dress," protested Lord Ranger. "We will return tomorrow."

They all saw the guests to the door and waved good-bye to them.

Lord Ranger picked up the reins and said to Lord Paul as they drove away, "Why so thoughtful, my friend?"

"They are an endearing pair of young ladies," said Lord Paul, "and have led quite a dreadful life. We should not add complications to it."

"Meaning, don't raise hopes of marriage?"

"No, I do not mean that. They are too unworldly to be socially ambitious. I mean, do not break any hearts, Ranger. As it is, they will have a hard enough time returning to their own world when Christmas is over."

"Look how the snow falls! Paul, I only know one thing. That child's heart will be broken if I do not take her sledging tomorrow."

"Miss Jilly is far from being a child," said his friend severely, but Lord Ranger had urged his team to a gallop and did not seem to hear.

* * *

Mandy and Jilly sat on Jilly's bed that night and told each other everything that had happened. With one exception. Mandy did not tell Jilly she had fallen in love.

Chapter Three

"AND JUST WHERE do you think our leaping lords are off to today?" demanded Lady Harriet to her friend, Lucinda, as they stood together at the window of Colonel Tenby's drawing room and watched Lord Ranger and Lord Paul loading a long sledge onto the roof of their carriage.

Snow covered the rolling parkland outside the colonel's mansion. The sight of the snow had cheered Harriet and Lucinda because they thought it would keep the gentlemen indoors to amuse them.

Harriet and Lucinda could have been taken for sisters instead of friends. Both were beautiful brunettes with liquid brown eyes, straight noses, and tiny mouths. For some reason, neither had "taken" during their last Season. Mrs. Tenby, who was a friend of both their parents and considered herself a clever matchmaker, had invited them as soon as her husband had told her about the visit of Lord Ranger and Lord Paul.

Harriet rang the bell by the fireplace, and when a footman answered its summons, she ordered, "Find out where Lord Paul and Lord Ranger have gone."

"They were at the Harringtons' last night and did not arrive home until the small hours," said

Lucinda. "Surely they cannot be going back there. What is the attraction in a couple of drabs?"

Harriet bit her lip in vexation. "Perhaps Sir John Harrington has other houseguests, *prettier* houseguests."

The footman returned. "Well?" demanded Harriet imperiously.

The footman, who was very tall and good-looking, bowed obsequiously low. "Lords Ranger and Paul have gone to Sir John Harrington's. A sledging party, I believe."

"Thank you, Peter," said Harriet, "that will be all."

When the footman had left, Lucinda sighed. "Such legs. I think he adores you, Harriet." And Harriet gave a little complacent smile.

"Mark my words," said the footman, Peter, in the servants' hall, "those chilly-faced antidotes will be off in hot pursuit."

"Do not speak like that of your betters," admonished the butler. "But Sir John's boy was in the kitchens the other day saying as how there are two pretty little misses in residence at Greenbanks."

"Do you think they will come?" asked Jilly.

"I do not know how many times you have asked me that," said Lady Harrington indulgently. "But do remember they are Colonel Tenby's houseguests, and he may have had something planned for them."

"Here they are!" cried Mandy from the window where she had been posted for the last hour. "And they have a sledge, a large sledge on the roof of their carriage."

"Go upstairs and change into your warmest clothes," ordered Lady Harrington. The girls ran out. Lady Harrington rang the bell, and when her maid answered it, she said, "Peg, go and help the young ladies dress warmly, but find two of my best bonnets for them, and make sure they do not wear their own. And tell them they must not stay out too long, for they have to be fitted for ball gowns and learn some more dance steps. Tell the schoolmaster and the curate to come for dinner. We can have some dancing after that."

Soon Lord Ranger, Lord Paul, Jilly, and Mandy were climbing the high hill above the pond. Lord Ranger looked up at the steely gray sky. "More snow, I think."

"Oh, I hope it snows and snows and snows," said Mandy in a quiet voice, "so that Ma and Pa can never come to take us away."

Lord Paul felt a tug of tenderness at his heart. "Enjoy today or you will spoil everything by worrying about the future," he said.

Lord Paul sat in front of the sledge with Mandy behind him, then Jilly and Lord Ranger at the back.

Lord Ranger gave the sledge a mighty push and then scrambled aboard and clutched Jilly's shoulders. The girls screamed with delight as the sledge hurtled downward. It must be like flying, thought Jilly. Then the sledge struck the ice of the pond, flew across it like an arrow, hit the bank on the other side, and sent them flying over the ice.

Lord Ranger stumbled to his feet and slid over to where Jilly was lying in a heap on the ice. He helped her to her feet, saying anxiously, "Are you all right?"

She turned a radiant face up to him. "That was so wonderful. May we go again?"

"Devils for punishment," laughed Lord Ranger, seeing that Mandy, too, was unhurt. "But your bonnets are sadly crushed."

"Oh, dear, not *our* bonnets," cried Jilly. "Lady Harrington's bonnets. Let us take them off and hang them on a branch, Mandy, so that we may not damage them further."

The men looked on, amused, as the girls unselfconsciously hung their bonnets on a branch. Then they all went up the hill again.

"Let's see if we can steer this thing properly," said Lord Ranger. "Off we go!"

But try as they might, the sledge once more flew straight across the ice of the pond like a bird, hit the bank, and sent them sprawling on the ice. The pins flew out of Jilly's red hair and it tumbled down her back.

They were laughing and slipping and helping one another up from the ice when they all became aware of Harriet and Lucinda, standing at the edge of the pond watching them.

"Dear me, what vulgar little hoydens do we have here," said Harriet to Lucinda. Both Harriet and Lucinda were wearing thick velvet dresses under fur-lined cloaks. Both carried fur muffs and had fur-lined bonnets out of which their disdainful faces stared at Jilly and Mandy.

Lord Ranger made the introductions. Jilly and Mandy immediately felt very young and gauche.

"Perhaps the Misses Davenport would allow us to take their places," suggested Harriet.

"By all means," said Jilly sadly. She and Mandy stood on the ice and watched as Lord Paul and Lord

Ranger courteously assisted Harriet and Lucinda up the hill with as much care as if they were made of glass.

Sir John's boy, Jimmy, who acted as page, knife boy, and pot scrubber, ran back to the house. "Oh, madam," he said to Lady Harrington, "two fashionable ladies have turned up and are spoiling the sledging party!"

Lady Harrington told him to get out the gig and then dressed as quickly as she could and drove herself down to the pond. Lord Ranger had not sent Harriet and Lucinda off with any tremendous push. The sledge had moved slowly down and then cruised gently over the ice.

"That was very pleasant," Lady Harrington heard Harriet say. "You will take us again."

"Just one more time," said Lord Paul. "This is the Misses Davenports' party."

"I am sure they don't mind a bit," Lucinda said, and turned away.

Lady Harrington scowled awfully. Mandy and Jilly looked so wistful. The red sun was setting behind the hills. Soon it would be dark.

She turned and saw Jimmy standing by the carriage. "Jimmy, run as hard as you can up that hill and give that sledge the biggest push you can."

"Right, my lady."

Jimmy was able to get ahead of the party because Lucinda and Harriet were taking mincing little steps up through the snow.

He crouched down behind a stand of trees and waited. Lord Ranger climbed on the back as he was not going to give the sledge any push and send it flying the way he had done with Jilly and Mandy.

Jimmy then flung himself forward and pushed it as hard as he could.

The sledge went hurtling forward. Lucinda and Harriet screamed and screamed. It hit the ice harder than it had ever done before, and all the occupants of the sledge were thrown out.

Harriet lay spread-eagle on the ice. A little way away from her lay Lucinda. With remarkable agility, Lady Harrington made her way across the ice, and before the gentlemen could reach them, she and Jilly and Mandy had raised Harriet and Lucinda to their feet.

"I am sure every bone in my body is broken," said Harriet. "We are not used to such hurly-burly games. *We* are used to behaving like ladies. Come, Lucinda."

They moved slowly to their carriage, where the footman, Peter, was already letting down the steps. Harriet and Lucinda did not suppose for a moment that the men would not accompany them. When they were driven off, they were quite confident that Lord Ranger and Lord Paul would be driving behind them.

"Are you unhurt?" asked Lucinda.

"Only in spirit. But we broke up that little party and showed those girls up for what they are. Did you see their clothes? And hatless. And hair tumbling everywhere. Enough to give any gentleman a disgust of them."

But when they alighted at Colonel Tenby's and looked back down the long, wintry drive in the fading light, there was no sign of Lord Ranger or Lord Paul.

"They have to load up that ridiculous sledge," said Lucinda. "They will be back soon, you'll see."

But when Harriet and Lucinda descended the stairs that evening for dinner in their very best gowns and wearing their very best jewels, they found to their fury that neither lord was present.

Jilly and Mandy did not know that Lord Ranger and Lord Paul had been prepared to follow Lucinda and Harriet but that Lady Harrington had taken them aside and said, "Do not spoil my ladies' fun. Lady Harriet and Miss Lucinda are, I am sure, used to all sorts of entertainments. So that things like this, which mean so very much to Jilly and Mandy, mean nothing at all to them." Both lords had then turned and surveyed the disconsolate Jilly and Mandy. Mandy's hair had come down as well and they both looked very young.

"Then we must not spoil their party," said Lord Ranger. "But it was most odd, Lady Harrington. I could swear that someone gave that sledge the most enormous push."

"Hardly," said Lady Harrington. "Who would do a thing like that? You are welcome to join us for dinner. We are informal this evening. No need to change."

She turned away before they could find time to refuse and then shouted back over her shoulder, "I shall tell Jimmy to ride over to Colonel Tenby with the news."

"Now, why do I feel we have been efficiently trapped?" said Lord Ranger. He and Lord Paul walked back to Mandy and Jilly. "Come, ladies, a few more times before we all die of cold."

Lord Paul saw the way their faces shone with pleasure. He could see no love light in Jilly's eyes and felt reassured. The fact that Mandy might have fallen for *him* never crossed his mind.

Jilly treasured every moment. They moved away to another hill which ended in a long, sloping field so there was no fear of hurts or spills.

Lord Ranger, who had considered himself long past enjoying such childish pleasures, was surprised to see Lady Harrington's Jimmy calling to them from the bottom of the hill that dinner would be served in an hour. He had not noticed the time pass.

They cruised down the hill and then Lord Ranger and Lord Paul pulled the two girls in the sledge back to the house.

Jilly and Mandy went upstairs to be fussed over by Peg, washed and dressed in more newly altered gowns, hair brushed and put up, and then downstairs again, faces glowing with health, looking forward to the evening.

Sir John saw nothing wrong in having the curate and the schoolmaster at his dinner table with two noble lords. Although both he and Lady Harrington hoped Lord Paul and Lord Ranger would instruct the girls in the intricacies of the new dance steps, the invitation to Mr. Parse and Mr. Tawst was not canceled as Sir John and Lady Harrington had kind hearts and knew that both men would be disappointed if the chance of a good dinner were snatched away from them.

Lord Paul was fastidious and hated sitting down at dinner in top boots and riding dress, which is what both he and Lord Ranger had chosen to wear for the sledging party. He told himself they would have been better off to return to Colonel Tenby's, where the company was elegant and the conversation witty. But he could not help finding the shy schoolmaster entertaining as the Harringtons skillfully drew him out to tell funny stories of the misdemeanors of the village boys. Soon Lord Paul forgot to be so high and mighty and was joining in the general conversation, flattered at the way little Mandy hung on his every word.

Dinner was slightly marred for Jilly when Sir John asked Lord Ranger about the two ladies he had heard had joined their party in the afternoon and Lord Ranger said easily that they were a couple of charmers who were houseguests of the Tenbys.' Jilly did not like that word *charmers*.

Mandy and she were wearing the sludge-colored gowns, but both had been embellished with soft collars at the low necklines of old lace, and Lady Harrington had lent Jilly a pearl necklace and Mandy a coral one. Apart from fob watches, the girls had never been allowed to wear jewelry before.

Sir John began to talk about Christmas. They followed German tradition, he said, by having a Christmas tree. A decorated tree had been a tradition in Germany since 1604, the Germans believing that Martin Luther first decorated the Christmas tree. The story goes that he was walking one Christmas Eve under a clear night sky lit by millions of stars, and the sight so moved him that he uprooted a fir tree and decorated its branches with candles to remind children of the heavens from which Christ descended. The King Georges of England were not only German, but had brought a lot of German settlers to England, particularly George II, who did not trust the British army and preferred his own troops. Some villages in England were still mostly German. So with them came the Christmas tree.

The Harringtons were determined to have a large fir tree along with the yule log, the holly and the ivy, and the mistletoe over the door.

Presents would be given—even the Puritans hadn't managed to stop that; it had been going on for so long, even the Romans exchanged gifts around what came to be known as Christmas.

Jilly and Mandy listened, wide-eyed with excitement, no thoughts of their parents' disapproval coming into their heads. There was so much about the Harringtons that their parents would disapprove of.

There was, of course, to be a Father Christmas, who would head the mummers on Christmas day, the mummers being the masked players. Father Christmas had been around since pagan times. The Puritans hadn't stamped him out, preferring to quench the praying to Saint Nicholas, a popish practice not to be encouraged, and so Father Christmas, with his white beard, his great belly, and his cudgel, reigned supreme.

And then Jilly thought about those Christmas presents and began to worry. She and Mandy certainly had pin money, not much of it, but enough to buy a few things. "What is troubling you?" asked Lord Ranger.

"I was thinking about Christmas presents and wondering how to get them," said Jilly.

He thought quickly. He was sure that the dreadful Davenports would not have furnished their daughters with enough money to buy anything expensive.

"We will be going to Oxford sometime next week

if the roads are not too bad. If you give me a list, I will see what I can do for you. There are plenty of shops around here, but I am sure you do not want to embarrass your host with anything too expensive. Grand gifts are not expected from young ladies. Did you know that?"

Jilly looked relieved. "No, I did not. It is most kind of you to offer to help. But I do not know what to give."

"Perhaps you might leave it to me?"

The minute the words were out of his mouth, he wondered what he was playing at. He had no desire to forge any bonds of intimacy with this chit. But the large green eyes turned up so trustingly to his were full of gratitude.

"Thank you, my lord. I will fetch you the money after dinner."

"There is no need for that." Something prompted him to say, "Paul and I have promised to take Lady Harriet and her friend to Oxford on a shopping expedition, so I am going there anyway."

Mandy overheard that remark and tried to keep a smile on her face and not show how depressed she was. Jilly felt a sharp stab of jealousy, but not sexual jealousy. She envied Harriet and Lucinda for being so very much a part of Lord Ranger's world, a world that they would continue to inhabit and enjoy long after she and Mandy had been taken back north to their old repressed life.

"Now, what has brought the shadows back into your eyes?" teased Lord Ranger.

"I find I am jealous of Lady Harriet and Miss Lucinda," said Jilly candidly.

He gave her a guarded look. "And why is that?"

"Because all this—" she waved an expressive

hand round the table "—all the balls and parties and merriment, are everyday things to them, but not to us."

"That is why you show such refreshing enjoyment in everything. Do you not know it is fashionable to be bored?"

"Why is it fashionable to be bored? Is that not an insult to one's hosts?"

"I think it all started away back at the court of Marie Antoinette. You know how slavishly we copy French fashion whether we are at war with the French or not. Well, it became the thing not to show any emotion at all, neither sadness nor happiness. The fashion came here, and here it stays.

Jilly's eyes flashed wickedly and then she composed her face into a bored mask. "Like so?"

"Yes, my imp. But I prefer you the way you are."

"Are you flirting with me, my lord?"

"Perhaps. You see, I am *very* fashionable."

Jilly gave her infectious gurgle of laughter.

Lord Paul helped Mandy to salad. "I hope my friend is behaving himself. He is rather a careless heartbreaker."

Mandy looked at him shyly. "And you, my lord?"

He laughed. "I am perhaps more responsible in my actions."

Sir John tapped his spoon against his glass. "I have not warned our guests, Lord Paul and Lord Ranger, of their fate this evening. We are endeavoring to teach the girls how to dance, and your help is requested after dinner."

"We can hardly dance in our boots," said Lord Paul.

Lord Ranger grinned. "We can take them off and allow the ladies the pleasure of treading on our stockinged feet."

The trouble about close friends is that they will sometimes never mind their own business. Lord Paul fretted that Lord Ranger was raising hopes of marriage in this household, and it was as well for Mandy that he was so busy concentrating on his friend's behavior that he did not notice the yearning look in Mandy's eyes. But Lady Harrington did and heaved a romantic little sigh. If nothing came of it, she thought, at least little Mandy would know what it had been like to be in love, and every young miss should know that. She herself had married Sir John against her parents' wishes. It was pointed out to her that he was a mere baronet with little money. Then a relative had died and had made him a very wealthy man, a state of affairs that Sir John accepted lazily, as he had accepted his previous lack of money.

At the end of the dinner, the curate said he would play for them and they all went through to the drawing room. There were no servants around to roll up the carpet, so they did it themselves and moved back the furniture.

Jilly thought she would never, ever forget that evening, not until the day she died. She learned to move gracefully in the waltz in Lord Ranger's arms under the low beams of the ceiling while the old dogs snored in front of the blazing fire and the curate played and played.

Mandy moved in a dream. For different reasons, she was savoring every moment. Love had given her quick perceptions she had never had before and a new maturity. She knew that Lord Paul liked her, had even become fond of her, but not only had he no intention of marrying her, he was determined that Lord Ranger's feelings for Jilly should never become anything warmer than friendship. So having decided to live for the minute and put all thoughts of romance out of her head, Mandy behaved charmingly and with a new confidence.

"What are you doing awake at this unearthly hour?" demanded Harriet, waking to find Lucinda sitting on the end of her bed at eleven in the morning.

"You have to get up," ordered Lucinda. "We must hold a conference with Mrs. Tenby. This is war. Peter, the footman, reported to me that our gallants arrived back from the Harringtons' at three in the morning, and in a high good humor, too. Are we to have two such prizes snatched from under our noses by a couple of provincials?"

And so an hour later, which was fast dressing for Harriet, saw the two of them closeted in Mrs. Tenby's boudoir. Mrs. Tenby was a plump, domineering woman with the sensitivity of an ox. She had overweening self-confidence and vanity. It seemed right to her that her guests should appeal to her for help. Despite the fact that she was American by birth, the democracy of that new country had passed her by, leaving her rigidly snobbish. She felt it would be a personal affront if two English lords, while under her roof, were taken away by undistinguished guests in another household.

"The point is," said Harriet, "that both men are at loose ends and so they entertain themselves by going over to the Harringtons'. Were we to produce lively amusements, skating parties and so on, they would have no reason to go elsewhere."

"My poor husband is not aware of my plans for you," said Mrs. Tenby, "so we will not trouble him with them, but he will do as he is told. Leave it to me!"

The colonel raised his head as his wife came into his study and tried not to look forward to the days after Christmas when he would be rejoining his regiment. He who had bravely faced the French *tirailleurs* at Waterloo was frightened of his domineering wife.

"I want you to tell the servants to sweep the lake," said Mrs. Tenby. "We are having a skating party this afternoon."

"Yes, dear."

"At three o'clock. And tell them to have lanterns placed around the edge of the lake because it becomes dark early. And a bonfire for warmth. And some tables along beside the lake with rum punch."

"Yes, dear."

After she had gone, the colonel rang for his butler and issued the orders. Then he said, "Send that footman, Peter, to me."

The colonel had suddenly decided that if he was to trudge around a freezing lake on a winter's afternoon, it might help to have some congenial company. It was ridiculous that he had not yet seen Sir John Harrington. He would send the footman over to Greenbanks with an invitation to the skating party. His wife could not possibly take exception, he thought naively, since the two most favored guests appeared to enjoy the company of the Harringtons.

Peter, the footman, listened to the instructions and wondered whether to warn his master, of whom he was very fond, that Mrs. Tenby would not approve, but decided against it. He had taken a strong dislike to Lady Harriet and Miss Lucinda and was gleefully looking forward to seeing their faces when the party from the Harrington household arrived.

"We shall go," said Sir John, reading the invitation aloud.

"But the fittings for the girls' ball gowns!" cried Lady Harrington. "Besides, I do not think it very politic to let Lord Paul and Lord Ranger see them alongside very fashionable people. They might appear to a disadvantage."

"They are going to the ball in Moreton, are they not? Better to get them used to such fashionable company first at an informal skating party."

"Nothing to do with Mrs. Tenby is ever informal. I cannot abide that woman. Poor Colonel Tenby. We must go. I think his invitation is a cry for help."

Her sharp eyes noticed that the invitation was not greeted with the usual cries of delight with which Jilly and Mandy normally heralded every suggestion. Jilly said primly that it sounded "very nice." Mandy said nothing, but her large blue eyes held a guarded look.

Everyone was skating beautifully on Colonel Tenby's ornamental lake. No shouts, no clumsy falling down, only decorous circling with the ladies.

Mrs. Tenby's efficiency had effectively tamed nature. The ice had been swept until it looked like black glass. Lanterns had been set geometrically six feet from one another around the lake. She had had Peter measure the distance. A table with a white cloth stood beside the lake with punch bowls and glasses. There was no unbridled bonfire; instead two fires burned in polished steel braziers. Armchairs, sofas, and footstools had been carried out from the house so that the guests could rest in the same comfort as they could in the drawing room.

Mrs. Tenby watched with satisfaction as Lord Ranger moved slowly around the ice with Harriet, and Lord Paul with Lucinda.

And then she saw a carriage rolling up the drive. "Who can that be?" she asked the colonel.

"Probably Sir John," he said easily. "Asked the Harringtons and their party over."

Mrs. Tenby's already highly rouged face went even redder with anger. "Fool!" she said bitterly, and strode off, leaving her husband looking after her in a bewildered way.

Jilly and Mandy, both at the same time, wished themselves elsewhere. It was more like a ball than a skating party. Everything was so calm and formal, the skates hissed over the ice, the fires crackled, but otherwise everything was as cold and silent as the winter weather.

But their very presence was already brightening the lives of two young men at the colonel's house party, Mr. Travers and Mr. Jensen. Both young men had initially tried to court Harriet and Lucinda but had been ruthlessly snubbed. They had not turned their attentions to any other ladies in the house party, for the rest appeared to want to emulate the cold, high-and-mighty manner of Harriet and Lucinda. They waited impatiently until Jimmy had strapped on Jilly and Mandy's shoes and helped them to the ice, and then they skated forward and bowed low. "May we take you ladies for a spin on the ice?"

Surprised and delighted not to be left alone, Jilly

and Mandy agreed, Jilly going off with Mr. Travers, and Mandy with Mr. Jensen.

"It is a bit like a funeral," said Jilly, after they had circled the ice slowly several times. "We were sledging yesterday and I liked that. I like going very fast."

Mr. Jensen and Mandy skated up to join them. "Miss Jilly," said Mr. Travers, who had found out her name, "says she likes to move very fast."

Mr. Jensen, a chubby young man with an endearing grin, said, "Then let's go as fast as we can. I know, we'll have a race!"

They lined up at the edge of the lake and then started off. The other skaters moved off the ice and stood watching as, shrieking and laughing, the girls with their partners raced each other round the lake.

"That looks like fun," said a Miss Charteris to her friend, Miss Andrews.

"Mrs. Tenby looks furious," pointed out Miss Andrews.

Miss Charteris pouted. "Mrs. Tenby is always furious about something. Those girls from Greenbanks look like *fun*.. I'm going to join them."

She skated up, followed by Miss Andrews, and caught Jilly round the waist. "Like a line of carriages," she shouted. Soon—with Mr. Travers leading, and Jilly hanging on to his waist, then Miss Charteris hanging on to Jilly, with her friend, Miss Andrews, behind, then Mr. Jensen and Mandy—they all snaked their way around the ice at great speed. One by one the other guests, laughing and shouting, caught on to the end of the line until the whole party, with the exception of the older members, along with Harriet, Lucinda, Lord Ranger, and Lord Paul, were sailing round the ice. Then Mr. Travers lost his footing and they all collided into one another and fell in a heap on the ice.

"Disgraceful," murmured Harriet. "Do you not think so, Lord Ranger?"

"They are young," he said, feeling about a hundred years old.

"I, too, am young," pointed out Harriet, who was nineteen, "and yet such rude displays are not those of a lady."

Lady Harrington had been talking to the colonel, who in turn called Peter, the footman, said something to him, and sent him off to the house. Peter returned carrying a fiddle and started to play a lively tune. The skaters moved off in time to the music while the lanterns round the lake were lit and the sun went down.

Lord Paul watched moodily as Mandy's little figure flew round and round. He was chafing at being kept so firmly anchored to Lucinda's side. But neither he nor Ranger could desert them and join the skaters. Both Lucinda and Harriet seemed content to stand elegantly at the edge of the lake, looking scornfully at the noisy party.

Lord Ranger glanced sideways at Harriet's beautiful face. It was strange, but he had always imagined himself eventually settling for a wife like this. She would run his home efficiently and always look mannered and beautiful. There was a scream from the ice as Jilly went spinning off and fell in a heap.

Not someone like that, he thought, but a smile curved his lips and he forgot about minding his manners and staying at Harriet's side, and skated quickly up to Jilly before Mr. Travers could reach her and pulled her to her feet. "You hoyden," he said. "Mrs. Tenby looks fit to have an apoplexy."

Her worried eyes flew to his face. "Have I done something wrong? You should have told me. You know I do not know how to go on."

"You have enlivened a dull party and made me forget my duty to Lady Harriet."

"Your *duty* to Lady Harriet? What duty, my lord?"

"Only that with you and your sister taking all the other guests away, I feel someone has to keep her company."

Jilly saw Mr. Travers hovering near and said quickly, "So you cannot skate with me?"

Hot punch was being served and the guests were all chattering and laughing and moving towards the table at the edge of the lake. Harriet, Lucinda, and Lord Paul were joining them.

"Now I can," he said. "Give me your hands. I think we have the ice to ourselves."

They skated around, gloved hands tightly holding gloved hands. Lord Ranger suddenly felt at peace with the world. It was as well he did not hear what Mrs. Tenby was saying to Lady Harrington.

"I must get my guests indoors," Mrs. Tenby was saying firmly. "I would invite you and your party to dinner, Lady Harrington, but I have not told the chef to expect other guests and so—"

"I would not dream of dining with you," said Lady Harrington. "Ah, Sir John, we must go."

He looked surprised, and beside him, the colonel's face registered dismay.

And so Jilly and Mandy were called away from the punch table. They cheerfully waved farewell, and Lord Ranger heard Jilly promising Mr. Travers a dance.

The Harrington coach rumbled off down the drive, seeming to take all the light and color out of the party with it.

"Now we can behave like grownups again," said Lady Harriet, and laughed. But no one joined in.

Had Lord Ranger and Lord Paul, despite their long military experience, not been such products of their class and age, it would have struck both forcibly that to be with the Davenport girls meant fun and laughter and to be with Harriet and Lucinda meant a certain amount of tedium. But even the younger sons of dukes were used to knowing their place and making sure no one encroached on it. They were also made aware from their birth what was due to their position. Lucinda and Harriet were "suitable," the Davenport girls were not. One did not only marry a lady but her family as well, and who wanted his fine old name to be tied to that of some dismal, repressive Yorkshire family without wit or elegance?

And so Lord Ranger flirted expertly that evening with Harriet, and Lord Paul with Lucinda. Both girls were practiced flirts, and their undoubted beauty was enough to quicken the senses. Lord Paul and Lord Ranger moved easily about the goldfish bowl of their own world and only remembered the Davenports when Mr. Travers yawned and said, "What a curst dull evening. Let's ride over tomorrow and see those Misses Davenport. Don't think Sir John will mind."

Miss Charteris and Miss Andrews promptly begged to be taken as well, and Lord Paul noticed the disappointed little exchange of glances between

Mr. Travers and Mr. Jensen before they gallantly agreed.

He was about to suggest to Lord Ranger that they go as well. He had not skated with Mandy and felt he should have been more courteous towards the girl. She was such a confiding little thing. But Mrs. Tenby smiled on them and said they had surely remembered that they were to take Lady Harriet and Miss Lucinda to Oxford.

Lord Ranger remembered Jilly had given him a little money to buy presents. At least he could do that for her.

Chapter Four

IN HER DREAMS, Mandy skated across the ice with Lord Paul. His black eyes glinted down into hers, he pressed her hands tightly. "I have something to tell you," he said. "I love . . . I love . . ."

"Me?" she cried. "Do you love me?"

A look of hauteur crossed his face. "No, Lucinda, I love Lucinda." And he released her hands and skated away from her. She could feel the ice beginning to crack under her. She called to him for help. But he skated farther and farther away.

She awoke with a scream. Jilly started up at the sound of her sister's voice and ran through to her bedchamber, crying, "Mandy! Mandy! What's amiss?"

Mandy struggled up against the pillows, her eyes shining with tears in the flickering light of the rush lamp in its pierced canister beside the bed. "A bad dream," she said in a choked voice. "Nothing more." She forced a weak smile. "What have I here to distress me?"

"Do you want me to stay with you until you sleep? I know. We have not had time to finish *Pride and Prejudice*. I will read to you."

And so Jilly read until Mandy's eyes began to

close, and finally, just after the last sentence of the book, she fell into a deep sleep.

Jilly rose and looked down at her sister. She wondered for the first time if something was wrong. Mandy swung between delight and sadness, her large eyes showing changing emotions like clouds' shadows chasing each other across a field. Jilly tried to banish the worry firmly from her mind as she went back to her own bed. Worry, she associated with home, and she refused to think of home and spoil this golden visit.

The girls were being fitted for their ball gowns the following day when Lady Harrington came in and said in an amused voice that four young people had come over from Colonel Tenby's and brought a sledge with them.

"Anyone else?" asked Mandy, pleating the thin material of her gown with nervous fingers.

Lady Harrington gave her a quick look of sympathy and said, "No. Would you have the whole of Mrs. Tenby's party here? She would never forgive me. Let's have these gowns off and go and enjoy yourself."

Colonel Tenby had locked himself in his study. He had endured the full force of his wife's wrath at bedtime the night before. How *dare* he ask Sir John and his party over? The colonel had replied with some force that Sir John was an old friend and a neighbor and he had thought those Davenport girls were utterly charming. This unexpected stand had left his wife speechless, but he knew she would return to the attack the next day, which was why he was sitting with his door locked as if awaiting an attack from the French.

But the little spark of rebellion that had started the day before was growing into a flame. He was on leave. He should be relaxing, not crouching behind the locked door of his study like a guilty child dreading punishment to come. He had been out walking earlier. His greatcoat was lying on a chair in the corner along with his hat, gloves, and scarf.

Almost without thinking, he went and put them on. He then went to the window and raised it and climbed out onto the terrace, and closed the window behind him. With one quick look round, he sprinted along the terrace and then began to make his way over the snowy lawns to the stables. He felt as cheerful as if he were setting out on a campaign as he swung himself up into the saddle and rode off down the drive.

As he rode toward Greenbanks, he could feel the feathery brush of snow on his cheeks, and then as the old house came in sight, he could hear shrieks and yells from the hillside above the house where the young people were sledging.

That flame of rebellion that had brought him this far was suddenly flickering. He felt unaccountably shy and not sure of his welcome.

Jimmy, the Harringtons' boy, appeared with a cheerful "Good day, sir. I'll take your horse to the stables. Sir John and Lady Harrington are in the drawing room."

The front door was open and a pretty maid was bobbing a curtsy. He could hardly retreat now. He squared his shoulders and walked in.

The drawing room when he was ushered in seemed to open its arms to engulf him in warmth and color. And there was Lady Harrington springing to her feet with a glad smile of surprise on her face, and Sir John, more lethargic, putting aside his newspaper and saying, "Well, this is a surprise and a very welcome one, too. You need a glass of mulled ale to put you to rights after your ride, Colonel."

The colonel had been schooled by his wife not to talk of military matters—"not suitable for polite company." And so he was gratified to be plied with questions about the Battle of Waterloo and had he met Napoleon and was the little Corsican as mad as they said? A glass of mulled ale in his hand and a roaring fire at his feet, the colonel began to talk, shyly at first, and then fired by the rapt attention of his listeners, he relived the battle and then began to talk of Napoleon. "I was disappointed," he said. "I thought him a petulant, shabby sort of fellow, but Wellington said his very presence on the battlefield was worth the strength of several regiments."

Back at the colonel's, Mrs. Tenby was rattling the study door furiously for the umpteenth time. "May I suggest, madam," said Peter, the footman, "that I walk along the terrace and look in the window and see if Colonel Tenby is all right?"

Her heavy face cleared. "Do that. I will wait here."

Peter went outside and along the terrace. He looked in the study window and a grin crossed his face as he saw it was empty. He lifted the window and climbed in and went and unlocked the door. "The colonel is not here, madam," said Peter.

"Not here? Not here! But how did he get out? And where has he gone?"

Peter, who had easily deduced that his beleaguered master had probably escaped by the window, stood wooden-faced and refrained from comment.

"Oh, go about your duties," snapped Mrs. Tenby. "See that there are enough logs in the drawing room."

Peter went to the drawing room, where a small group of people were sitting about, looking bored. "Where's Travers and Jensen, not to mention Miss Andrew and Miss Charteris?" asked one young man.

"I understand they have taken a sledge and gone over to the Harringtons'," said Peter, taking logs out of the basket and building up the fire.

"Lucky them," said the young man moodily. "Wish I'd thought of that. Dead as the grave here."

"You will find, sir, if I may say so," said Peter, delicately laying the idea on their bored minds as he laid a log on top of the blaze, "that it is not too late to join them, and the Harringtons are very easygoing, welcoming people."

The young man stood up. "I'm going." There was a chorus of "Wait for us."

"There are some sledges in the tack room," said Peter. "It would be a good idea to take some more."

So Mrs. Tenby, after driving about the estate searching for her missing husband, returned to find that a large number of guests had disappeared as well. She could only content herself with the thought that Lucinda and Harriet were in Oxford with Lord Ranger and Lord Paul.

* * *

Lord Ranger and Lord Paul were having a pleasant day. Both Lucinda and Harriet had been schooled all their young lives to please and flatter men. They were comfortably aware of the admiring stares they received as they went from shop to shop, of the quizzing glasses raised in their direction when they dined at The Mitre in the High Street.

They were disappointed when the falling snow, although light, prompted the gentlemen to make an early start home. Lord Ranger had made several purchases for Jilly and Mandy, but apart from that, had not thought of them much.

By the time the carriages turned in at the drive of the Tenbys', the snow was beginning to fall heavily. There was no wind and large flakes circled lazily down.

Mrs. Tenby was there in the hall to meet them with a glad smile and to tell them that they had time to change and dress as dinner had been set back especially for them.

"We did very well," said Harriet after she had finished dressing and had walked through to Lucinda's room, which adjoined her own. "Our gentlemen were vastly taken with us."

Lucinda gave a pleased little smile. "Not a mention of those hoydens over at Greenbanks. I do not think we will be plagued with them again."

Arms round each other's waists, they went down to the drawing room and then stood in the doorway and looked into the room with surprised expressions on their faces. Apart from themselves and Lord Ranger and Lord Paul, there were no young people. "Where is everyone?" asked Harriet, moving into the room.

"The young people have gone over to Sir John's,"

said Mrs. Tenby. "They should have been back by now. Oh, what is it, Peter?"

The footman bowed and handed her a note on a silver tray. "Jimmy, the Harringtons' boy, has just brought this over."

Mrs. Tenby scanned the note and then her face darkened. "It seems that my guests have decided to stay with the Harringtons this night because of the weather."

"Where is Colonel Tenby?" asked Lord Ranger, who was fond of his host.

"He has decided to stay at Greenbanks as well."

Lord Ranger looked around the glittering drawing room with its many mirrors and gilt furniture. In the shabby drawing room at Greenbanks, the carpet would be rolled back. There would be dancing or playing games. Jilly's odd green eyes would be shining with pleasure and excitement and happiness, a happiness that seemed to fill the room.

Lord Paul wondered what Mandy was doing. He hoped such as Jensen and Travers were behaving themselves. Mandy was so innocent and trusting, such a child. She needed someone to look after her. She needed to learn to behave like Lucinda, pretty and correct on all occasions.

So why did the day they had just spent in such beautiful and correct company appear insipid, rather like a boring play?

Lord Ranger was thinking for the first time rather wistfully about his army days, of the easy camaraderie and the jokes and the laughs. Why that should come into his mind when he was so relieved to be free of battles, he did not know, but as he led Harriet into the formal splendor of the dining room, he found himself wondering how early he could retire from the company and go to his room and read.

Jilly was probably laughing and dancing with Travers, he thought as he sat down opposite Harriet. Jilly really did not know how to go on. She would stumble during the quadrille and fall against him. Harriet would never do such a thing. He had never thought of a wife in terms of passion. Ladies were not supposed to be capable of passion. Jilly and Mandy would not know that. They were a pair of unworldly innocents who would give their hearts and affections as freely and unself-consciously as they gave their warmth and laughter. How insipid this food made by the Tenbys' French chef tasted. How was it that the Harringtons' cook managed to make everything taste so delicious?

"What dark thoughts are preoccupying you?" asked Harriet.

"Thoughts of you," he answered automatically, and she raised her fan to her face and flirted with her eyes over the fringed edge of it.

Jilly and Mandy were amazed the way the Harringtons' household easily adapted to fit all these new guests. The dining table was extended and the food was as hot, delicious, and plentiful as ever, the maids carrying in the dishes and leaving the guests to help themselves in the old-fashioned way. At the Tenbys', the dishes were carried round to each guest by liveried footmen.

The noise was immense as all the young people chattered and laughed. Then Sir John interrupted to say that he found Colonel Tenby's description of the Battle of Waterloo fascinating, and the gratified colonel was immediately plied with questions.

There was no Mrs. Tenby to frown and say that no one wanted to hear about war. He blossomed under the attention, and Jilly and Mandy sat with their hands clasped, drinking in every word.

After dinner there were games of charades, and, of course, the Harringtons had a large trunk full of all sorts of different costumes. Then there was dancing, and Lady Harrington was delighted to notice how well the girls' dancing had improved.

Jilly had almost forgotten about Lord Ranger, that tall and disturbingly handsome man. Mr. Travers was such free and easy company, and he was her own age. Miss Charteris and Miss Andrews, now on first-names terms as Belinda and Margaret, were such friendly, unself-conscious girls, and not at all like Harriet and Lucinda. The only thing to mar Jilly's evening was the occasional sad look in Mandy's eyes.

They did not retire to bed until three in the morning. Jilly followed Mandy into her room. "What is the matter, sis?"

"What should be the matter, Jilly? We are having such a splendid time."

"But at times, even during the dancing, you looked sad, Mandy. I know that this all must end, we both know it. But we must put it out of our minds and enjoy each minute. Why spoil the present by worrying about the future?"

"It is not that," said Mandy. She sat down at the toilet table and began to brush out her long hair. Jilly stood beside her, and both their reflections were framed by the oval of the glass.

"What is it?" asked Jilly quietly. "We were never really able to talk together before we came here, you know. We were only just beginning to get to know each other, and I . . . I love my little sister, very much."

Tears welled up in Mandy's blue eyes and spilled down her cheeks.

Jilly took the brush gently from her hand and set it on the toilet table. "Tell me," she said.

Mandy raised her skirt and tugged a handkerchief out of her garter and mopped her eyes.

"I am in love, Jilly."

"In *love*?"

"With Lord Paul."

"Oh, Mandy, we are so inexperienced in the ways of the world, but one has only to see Lord Ranger and Lord Paul with Harriet and Lucinda to know that they are both very accomplished flirts. They are charming gentlemen and have been kind to us, but you will ruin this Christmas holiday with hopes and yearnings that can never come to anything."

"I cannot do anything about it," said Mandy in a tired little voice. "I have caught the infection of love and must let the illness run its course."

In vain did Jilly try to reason with her. But Mandy became more composed and agreed, yes, she would try to forget all about it, but something in the back of her eyes belied the hopeful statement.

Jilly went through to her own room and undressed and got into bed. She lay staring up at the canopy. If only this hadn't happened! And then she had a sudden bright vision of Lord Ranger's handsome face. His blue eyes glinted down at her.

She threw herself on her side and closed her eyes tightly. One of them being miserable was enough!

Lucinda and Harriet had decided on a plan before going to bed. Keeping Lord Ranger and Lord Paul away from their rivals might not be the answer. Besides, Harriet had overheard Lord Ranger say he had some things he had bought for Miss Jilly in Oxford and meant to ride over to Greenbanks. "We must go as well," said Harriet. "By our very elegance and beauty, we will expose how unsuitable those Davenport girls are."

Lord Paul and Lord Ranger were surprised to find Harriet and Lucinda standing in the hall, awake and dressed to go out at eleven in the morning, an hour when they were both usually asleep.

"We have decided to accompany you," said Lucinda, drawing on a pair of lavender kid gloves. And confident of their welcome, both girls moved towards the doorway.

"We are both riding," said Lord Ranger. "I do not know if the roads will allow a carriage to get through."

"Then we shall change into our riding dress," said Lucinda.

And without waiting for an answer, both ladies went back upstairs.

"Perhaps we should take the carriage after all," said Lord Ranger. "The sun is quite hot and Greenbanks is not very far."

But for some reason he could not quite fathom, Lord Paul was suddenly impatient to reach the Harringtons'.

"If we take the carriage," he said, "we might find part of the road impassable. If we take the carriage, the ladies will promptly keep us waiting further by putting on their carriage gowns, and if we have to return, they will then change back into their riding dresses and we will never get there."

"Well, that's one thing about the ladies," said

Lord Ranger "always keep you waiting. I'll send someone to the stables to get a couple of mounts for them."

He walked away and therefore did not hear his friend's acid remark. "Lay you a monkey the Davenport girls wouldn't keep us waiting."

An hour later, Lucinda and Harriet came down the stairs, elegant in the latest thing in riding dresses and blissfully unaware that both gentlemen were thoroughly cross with them.

Lord Paul felt as they rode out past the lodge gates that the whole day had been ruined, and he wished now that they were not going. Instead of a hard gallop with Lord Ranger, he was forced to slow his mount to a slow amble to fall into line with the ladies.

By the time he saw the low, sprawling length of Greenbanks at the foot of the hill, he could bear it no longer. "See you at the house," he said suddenly, and spurring his horse, he rode off in front of them.

Lord Ranger, following at a sedate pace, envied him.

Lord Paul found the company seated in the dining room, having a cold collation. His eyes flew immediately to Mandy, who was listening intently to something Mr. Jensen was saying and did not appear to be aware of his arrival, even though Sir John called out, "Take a chair, Lord Paul, you are most welcome."

Everyone was laughing and chattering, and Colonel Tenby looked years younger.

And then Lord Ranger, Lucinda, and Harriet came into the room. Lady Harrington's welcome was cut short as Harriet, with raised eyebrows, looked around the room and said, "We should like to retire and have our gowns brushed, if you please, Lady Harrington."

And so Lady Harrington had to leave the company, and Mr. Travers said quite audibly, "Now the frost has arrived, I suppose the fun will stop."

"What frost?" asked Sir John. "It is a fine day. Are you sledging today?"

"What do you think, Colonel?" asked Mr. Travers. "Will Mrs. Tenby expect us back?"

"Oh, I think if we are all back in time for dinner, that will do very well," said the colonel.

There were cries of delight from the young people. Everyone with the exception of Lord Paul, Lord Ranger, the colonel, and Sir John and Lady Harrington went off to get dressed.

Only about ten minutes later Lord Paul and Lord Ranger heard their cries and shouts from outside. The sledging party was off, and it was half an hour later when Lucinda and Harriet entered the dining room.

"Where is everyone?" asked Harriet.

"They have gone sledging. Do have something to eat, ladies," said Sir John.

Harriet and Lucinda exchanged complacent little smiles. Lord Ranger and Lord Paul had not gone with the sledging party: they had waited for *them*.

It did not cross their vain minds that both men, having escorted them over, could hardly go off and leave them.

Conversation became formal and stilted. This was not helped by Lady Harrington, who was cleverly trying to make everything seem as dreary as possible. She did not like Harriet or Lucinda, and besides, she had a dream of presenting the terrible

Davenport parents with the news of their daughters' engagements to Lord Ranger and Lord Paul.

How slowly Harriet and Lucinda ate, marveled Lord Paul. Faintly he could hear the shouts and cheers of the sledging party. That young Jensen fellow appeared vastly taken with Mandy, but he was a clumsy chap, not suitable for such a sensitive girl.

At last both ladies, after having pointedly looked around for napkins, that newfangled fashion not yet adopted by the Harringtons, sighed, exchanged rueful little smiles, and wiped their mouths delicately on the tablecloth.

"Perhaps you would care to join the sledging party?" suggested Lord Paul.

Harriet shook her head. "I have decided to give up such childish games."

Suddenly impatient, Lord Ranger got to his feet. "Then I must be in my second childhood. I shall not be long."

Lord Paul stood up and bowed to Harriet and Lucinda. "Excuse us," he said. And almost as if they dreaded being called back, both men quickly left the room.

Lady Harrington rose to her feet. "Come through to the drawing room fire, ladies."

Harriet and Lucinda, outwards meek and biddable, inwardly fuming, followed her.

"I have some things to attend to," said Lady Harrington, "but you will find some of the latest magazines just arrived from London, and ring the bell if there is anything else you want."

"This is infuriating," said Harriet, once they were alone.

"Not the way we planned it, and unless we can put a spoke in the Davenport girls' wheels, they, not us, might turn out to be the most popular at this dreary provincial dance in Moreton."

"Did you see their ball gowns?" asked Harriet, for they had been given Jilly's room to groom themselves in, and the two nearly finished ball gowns were on stands by the window. "Made by the local dressmaker. I looked at her clothes. All made over. Some of the ones that haven't been touched yet are dowdy in the extreme."

Harriet suddenly sat up straight. "I wonder if they have anything else that they would be able to use as ball gowns."

"I shouldn't think so. Why?"

"If anything were to happen to those gowns, then they could not go."

"We couldn't . . . could we?"

Harriet's eyes gleamed. "If you were to pretend to be faint, Lady Harrington would urge us to retire. Once we are up there, we will think what to do. So look faint!"

Lucinda promptly lay back in her chair with one limp hand to her brow. It was typical of this slovenly household, thought Harriet, that Lady Harrington should answer the bell herself.

Although Lady Harrington evinced great concern, she thought privately that the two girls were sulking. There was something so stagy about Lucinda's pose, as if that young lady were striking an Attitude. But she suggested that they retire abovestairs where her maid would apply lavender water to Lucinda's temples.

Lucinda endured the ministrations of the maid and then sent her away. No sooner was the door closed than she sat up. Both girls looked at those ball gowns.

"What do you think?" asked Harriet.

Lucinda swung her legs out of bed. Both stood side by side, looking at the dresses, which gleamed white in the fading light. Then Harriet lit a branch of candles with a taper thrust into the fire. She held the candles up.

"Now, say you were to take these candles from me, Lucinda," she said in a thoughtful voice. "Say you were to become faint and stagger towards these gowns. Oops! The gowns catch fire, but we do not want to burn down the house, so I grab a jug of water from the toilet table and pour it over them. Result, a total wreck."

"Let's do it," said Lucinda. She took the branch of candles and held the flickering flames against the dresses. The result was startling. Both gowns burst into flames.

Harriet doused them in water and then smothered the remaining flames with the bedcover, shouting, "Help! Help!" at the top of her voice.

The sledging party, just returning, heard those cries and they all scrambled to get upstairs to see what was the matter.

Lady Harrington and her maid were there before them. Lucinda was white and sobbing: she really did have a fright.

"Poor Lucinda," cried Harriet. "She fainted and knocked the candles over the gowns. Oh, what a disaster."

"A disaster indeed," said Jilly. Mandy stood rigid in the doorway, her eyes wide with shock and dismay. In her dreams she had danced in that gown, floated in Lord Paul's arms in that gown.

"Were those your gowns for the ball?" asked Margaret.

Jilly nodded dumbly.

"How fightful!" cried Belinda. "Do you have others?"

Jilly shook her head, still too miserable to speak.

Lord Ranger edged the little group aside and went and stood next to the ruined dresses. He stood and studied them for a moment. He looked down at the now-extinguished branch of candles lying on the floor. "How did the candles get over here?" he asked abruptly.

"Lucinda picked them up from the mantelpiece and was carrying them to the toilet table when she became faint and staggered across the room. Lady Harrington, Lucinda and I will be happy to pay you for their loss," said Harriet.

"I think it would be a greater help if you lent the girls two of your own ball gowns," said Lady Harrington.

Harriet's eyes widened and then she said, "But we only have one gown each."

There was a little silence. Lord Ranger exchanged a long look with Lord Paul. It was hard to believe that two such fashion plates, whose vast amount of luggage was still the talk of Colonel Tenby's servants, should have only one ball gown each.

Margaret turned to her friend, Belinda. "I have a gown I could spare, and Miss Jilly and I are of a height, and Miss Mandy could fit one of your gowns."

"Yes, I could do that," said Belinda.

"You are both Trojans," cried Mr. Travers in delight, and Margaret felt her generous gesture had been the right one, for Mr. Travers was really looking at her for the first time.

Lady Harrington turned round and found Jimmy at her elbow. "Get the carriage," she ordered. "I gather Lady Harriet and Miss Lucinda rode over. They must not ride back. Lord Paul and Lord Ranger can lead their horses back later."

"I am sure both gentlemen will wish to escort us home," flashed Harriet, "considering that Lucinda is still far from well."

"I shall go with you myself," said Lady Harrington firmly. "No, not another word. And I shall suggest to Mrs. Tenby that you are given a strong purge."

Harriet and Lucinda looked appealingly at Lord Paul and Lord Ranger, but both men had turned away.

Nearly crying with rage and disappointment, both ladies were marched to the door by Lady Harrington, who said over her shoulder, "I do feel the rest of you should be thinking of returning as well or Mrs. Tenby will never forgive me."

Lord Ranger turned around. "The rest of you go ahead. I have some business to transact with Miss Jilly."

Margaret and Belinda, after many fond farewells and protestations of friendship, got into the carriage with Mr. Travers and Mr. Jensen.

"You know what I think," said Mr. Travers as the carriage lurched homewards over the snow ruts in the road. "I think that cat, Lucinda, deliberately set light to those gowns."

"That was one of the main reasons we offered our own gowns," said Margaret.

Mr. Travers beamed at her. "You did splendidly," he said, and Margaret glowed.

"Besides," said Mr. Jensen, "it would be fine of you to take the gowns over tomorrow in person, and we could go with you."

"The Davenport girls are such fun," said Belinda generously. "And *I* think Lord Ranger and Lord Paul think so, too."

"And *I* think you are both fun yourselves," said Mr. Jensen, who had quite forgotten about Mandy already and was wondering if he could dare to give Belinda's hand a warm squeeze when he helped her down from the carriage.

In the drawing room, Jilly was looking at the presents Lord Ranger had brought. She and Mandy were alone with Lord Paul and Lord Ranger. The rest of the young people had left with Colonel Tenby, Lady Harrington had not yet returned from the Tenbys', and Sir John had retired to take a nap. "The scarf would do very well for Lady Harrington," Lord Ranger was saying, "and the new slippers for Sir John. The other trinkets are for the maids, and the knife is for Jimmy, the boy."

"How clever of you," said Jilly. "Did you have enough money?"

"Exactly right," replied Lord Ranger, thinking how unworldly Jilly was. The money she had given him had not even paid for the silk scarf.

"It is a pity about your gowns," he went on. "Were they very fine?"

"Lady Harrington said the muslin, which was all she could get locally, was too coarse, but they looked so grand to us," said Jilly wistfully. "How could Miss Lucinda be so clumsy?"

Mandy clenched her little hands into fists. "I do not think she fainted at all," she said. "All our closets have been gone through, Jilly, everything turned over, and not much attempt made to put things back the way they were."

Jilly threw her a warning look. She felt that Mandy would not endear herself to Lord Paul by criticizing Lucinda.

"I must thank you again for shopping for us," she said firmly. "I suppose you must soon be leaving as well?"

Lord Ranger stretched his long legs out to the fire and gave a little sigh. "There is no hurry," he said. "It is comfortable here. I know. Do you have any cards?"

"Playing cards? I believe there is an old pack in the drawer over there," said Jilly.

"Have you ever played cards?" asked Lord Paul.

"We were never allowed to," said Mandy.

"Oh, all young ladies should know how to play a simple game of cards."

Jilly rose and went and rummaged in the desk and came back with a pack. Her green eyes glinted. "Are you going to teach us?"

Lord Ranger smiled and nodded.

Lady Harrington gently pushed open the door of the drawing room half an hour later. Lord Ranger, Lord Paul, Jilly, and Mandy were seated around a rickety card table, which they had placed in front of the fire. Mandy was scowling ferociously down at her cards, and Lord Paul was watching her with a look in his eyes that Lady Harrington could not fathom, but she retired and quietly closed the door.

She went upstairs and roused her sleeping husband. "We have two extra for dinner," she said triumphantly.

"Who? What?" he demanded groggily.

"We have Lord Ranger and Lord Paul. They did not go back with those two awful cats, who, if you ask me, ruined those gowns deliberately, and if they think they have heard the last of it, they have not. I am sending Lady Harriet's parents a bill, for the gowns and for the ruined carpet."

Sir John blinked up at her. "That's a bit hard, ain't it? Women are always fainting."

"I tell you, that was deliberate, but it was worth it, for I think it has given our lords a disgust of them. Do you think it would be too pushing if I sent Jimmy over to Colonel Tenby's with a request that their night rails and evening clothes be packed up and brought back? Well, perhaps not their evening clothes, for a certain informality leads to intimacy, don't you think?"

"I think it's all headed for disaster," said Sir John. "They are both fine fellows and were, I believe, brave soldiers. But they will marry their own kind if they marry at all, and not two young misses with dreadful Puritan parents who probably have supplied them with very little dowry."

"Why? The Davenports are very rich."

"And mean with it. But do what you like, my sweeting. You always do."

By the time both guests sat down to dinner, they took the news that Lady Harrington had sent for their night clothes and a change of linen with equanimity.

Jilly was worried. Lord Paul, his black eyes dancing, was flirting very cleverly with Mandy, and Mandy's eyes were like stars. What would happen at the ball when she saw him dancing off with Lucinda? For Jilly was very much of Sir John's opinion that both men would marry their own kind if they married at all.

So when Lord Ranger smiled at her and said she was looking remarkably beautiful, she said curtly,

"Fustian. There is no need to flirt with me, my lord. Such a very *uncomfortable* thing to do when you don't mean a word of it." And Lord Ranger noticed that Jilly looked severely at Lord Paul as she said it.

Now instead of Lord Paul worrying about Lord Ranger, it was the other way around. Lord Ranger felt protective about the girls. If Mandy became spoony about Paul, it would ruin her Christmas.

But he said with automatic gallantry to Jilly, "On the contrary, I meant every word of it," and his eyes began to dance when she looked straight at him and said, "Pooh!"

"You have to be kind to me," said Lord Ranger. "You are in my debt for life. You lost ten thousand pounds to me at cards."

"You will need to take me to court, my lord, for I have no intention of paying you."

He dropped his voice. "You could pay me in kind."

"Barter, my lord?" She put her chin on her hand and regarded him thoughtfully. "What do I have that you want?"

His gaze dropped to her soft pink mouth. "Your lips."

He cursed himself immediately the words were out, for her face flamed almost as red as her hair.

"Forgive me," he said contritely. "I am a hardened flirt."

The color died out of Jilly's face and she said in a sad little voice, "I know. You are both flirts."

"I thought every woman loved a rake," he teased.

"Not this one," said Jilly. "Oh, you are spoiling this evening with your nonsense. Shall we play cards again after dinner? I am sure I am beginning to understand it, and I do want to win that money back."

"You shall have your revenge," he promised.

And so they played again after dinner while Lady Harrington knitted in the corner and her son, James, his wife, and baby, who had been visiting neighbors, returned to join them.

I would like a home like this, thought Lord Ranger suddenly. And the children would not be confined to the nursery either. But where would he find a wife like Lady Harrington, who seemed to take unexpected guests in her stride and who filled the very rooms with her own generous personality?

And then his eyes fell on Jilly. She was bending over her hand of cards. A loose red curl lay on her cheek. One of the old dogs lumbered up and put its heavy head on her knee, and she reached down and patted it. She had a rare beauty, he mused. One kept discovering bits of it each time. There was first of all the glory of her hair and eyes. Then there was the soft swell of that young bosom, then the slim curve of the hip. Her animation, her joy in everything, gave her grace and color.

Jilly looked up suddenly and their eyes met. She felt she was drowning in that gaze, slipping down into a world of feelings where she had no control.

"Pay attention to your game, my lord," she said, but she played very badly for the rest of the evening, even worse than before, and rose from the table owing Lord Ranger fifty thousand pounds.

Chapter Five

MARGARET, BELINDA, and their escorts, Mr. Travers and Mr. Jensen, arrived the following day, the girls bringing ball gowns with them.

Jilly and Mandy were in raptures over the pretty muslin dresses. Jilly's was pale green, and Mandy's, pale blue. The delight in being able to wear colors, in admiring the fine stitching and embroidery, made both of them give Belinda and Margaret impulsive hugs. And the only thing to dim the rest of the day for Jilly and Mandy was the absence of Lord Paul and Lord Ranger. When they went skating in the pond, now a circle of black glass surrounded by sparkling white snow, Jilly and Mandy's eyes kept straying in the direction of the road, both hoping to hear the sound of horses' hooves. There was no reason for them not to come. The bright sunlight of yesterday had melted the snow on the roads. Now all they had to worry about was that it would snow again before the ball and that they would be unable to reach Moreton-in-Marsh.

Jilly thought a lot about Lord Ranger, about the way their eyes had met. She did not want to end up as worried and longing as Mandy and kept trying to turn her mind to other things. But he seemed to have become *stamped* on her mind: his eyes, his smile, the light tan of his skin and the strength of his hands.

If only something would happen to Harriet and Lucinda to stop them from going to that ball. Jilly was in no doubt that the ruin of the ball gowns had been deliberate. At least they had shot their bolt. After such a dreadful thing, they would not dare try anything else.

But Harriet and Lucinda had a powerful ally in their hostess. Mrs. Tenby could not believe that her normally biddable and meek husband had defied her by staying at the Harringtons'. Such a thing had never happened before. Mrs. Tenby blamed those Davenport girls for having introduced vulgarity into her well-ordered life. Neither Harriet nor Lucinda had any intention of telling Mrs. Tenby that they had set those gowns on fire deliberately. They had explained it was a sad accident and Lady Harrington had not been at all sympathetic.

"I think we must put our cards on the table," said Mrs. Tenby firmly. "You seem to fear that these dowdy little misses are taking up the attention of Lord Paul and Lord Ranger."

Harriet sighed. "Gentlemen can be such fools."

"And who knows that better than I?" said Mrs. Tenby waspishly. "But surely with your looks and elegance, you will eclipse such as the Davenport girls."

"They are become very popular," admitted Lucinda, "in the way that little children and puppies are popular. Nothing too serious, mark you, but enough to give our lords the impression that they are highly favored. If only we could stop them from coming."

"Our Mr. Nash, who organizes the assemblies at the White Hart, is a friend of mine," said Mrs. Tenby thoughtfully.

"Can hardly be Beau Nash," drawled Harriet. "He's been in his grave this age."

"No, it was not the famous master of ceremonies of Bath," said Mrs. Tenby. "Perhaps I could persuade him to send a message to the Davenport household that the ball is canceled."

Lucinda's eyes gleamed, but then she gave a little sigh. "Travers and Jensen would give the lie to that."

"Wait a bit." Mrs. Tenby sat for a few moments in silence. "I have it," she said. "I will organize an entertainment for the day of the ball to keep everyone here. On the very day of the ball, Mr. Nash will send word to the Davenport household that the ball has been canceled owing to damage to the floor or something."

"But news travels fast in a country district," Harriet pointed out. "The Harringtons will hear the next day that the ball took place."

"Deepest apologies from Mr. Nash. He will say he thought he told them at the last minute as he had told everyone else that the ball was to go ahead after all."

"They won't believe that for a moment!"

"They'll have to believe it," said Mrs. Tenby. "Mr. Nash is a highly respected member of the community, and why should he lie? I will go and see him now."

Mr. Nash was the self-appointed king of fashion of Moreton-in-Marsh and the area around it. He was a bachelor of forty, small and fussy, and used his considerable fortune in slavishly following every vagary of fashion. His hair was frizzed up on top of his head, giving him a perpetual air of surprise, his waist was nipped in, his coattails reached to his ankles, and his shirt points were so high and so cruelly starched, it was easy to see why such a fashion had earned the nickname of Patricides.

Like most weak and effeminate men who have been brought up by domineering and bullying mothers, he gravitated to such as Mrs. Tenby. He thought her "very maternal," although the childless Mrs. Tenby was anything but.

But he fairly goggled at her when he heard her request. "But my deah Mrs. Tenby," he cried. "I would lose my reputation! Only think when it gets out that the ball has taken place after all."

"It is quite easy," said Mrs. Tenby impatiently. "All you do is tell Sir John when you next meet him that the servant you dispatched with the news that the ball was to take place after all got drunk and fell in the snow."

"Lady Harrington won't believe that for a moment," he said huffily. "Very downy one is Lady Harrington."

"Look here, the Harringtons are a careless, slipshod couple. After a momentary spasm of irritation, they will forget about it. I see you need further convincing. Do you know that K'ang Hsi *famille verte* plate I have in the Yellow Saloon?"

Mr. Nash licked his thin lips and nodded. Fine porcelain was his passion.

"Do this little thing for me and it is yours."

He hesitated only a moment. "Very well."

"Now," said Mrs. Tenby, almost half to herself,

"all that is left is for me to find a way of keeping the house party at home on the day of the ball."

Unaware of the plot that had been hatched to stop them going, Jilly and Mandy felt the fates were smiling on them as the day of the ball dawned bright and fair with a hard frost. The days of sunshine had melted the snow from the roads but kept the fields still glittering white. Everything sparkled like their eyes and their hearts.

The fact that they had not seen anyone from Colonel Tenby's heightened rather than diminished the anticipation.

Lady Harrington, kind and amused, said that it was only a little country ball. James and his wife, Betty, said they would not be going. But nothing could damp the girls' spirits.

"I am getting worried," Lady Harrington confided to her husband. "You know what these Moreton balls are like—Nash posturing and mincing about, pretending to be Beau Brummell. Bad refreshments and a lumpy floor. Our girls have done well at their dancing lessons, but mark my words, those two cats will be out to outdance them, and they will!"

"It will be all right," said Sir John in his usual lazy way. "They haven't been to a ball before. It will all seem wonderful to them."

"I am beginning to wish Paul and Ranger at the devil," said his wife. "Travers and Jensen are more our girls' weight, and they're *young*. Paul and Ranger are in their early thirties and, if you will forgive the crudity, my heart, have probably had more women between them than I have had hot dinners, and I must be mad to be trying to throw my ewe lambs at their feet."

"Not *your* daughters," said the colonel placidly.

"Wish they were," muttered his unrepentant wife. "Dear God, I wish it *would* snow. I wish something would happen to stop them going to this ball."

"Beg pardon, my lady," said a maid, bobbing a curtsy, "but there's a messenger here from Mr. Nash."

"Send him in."

A tall, thin footman wearing Mr. Nash's livery—pink plush heavily laced with gold braid—minced in, bowed so low, his nose nearly touched the floor, and then handed over a sealed letter with many flourishes. In fact, Lady Harrington, trying to take the letter from him, thought at one moment that he was playing a game with her and that she was expected to leap up in the air and snatch it like getting the ball in a child's game.

She broke open the seal and scanned the contents. "Dear me," she said to her husband. "How very odd. The ball has been canceled. Part of the floor has caved in with dry rot."

But she felt like some great sort of candle snuffer when she went later to break the news to Jilly and Mandy. What glowing faces they turned to her as she walked into Jilly's room. What dismay and depression looked out of their eyes when she told them her news. She felt guilty because she had wished only such a short time ago that something would happen to stop them going to the ball, and now it had.

"There will be other parties," said Lady Harrington. "We will have a dance here on Christmas day, and I will ask Belinda and Margaret to let you have the dresses until then." Jilly and Mandy looked sadly at the gowns spread out on the bed in all their wonderful prettiness.

After Lady Harrington had left with many assurances that they would have a relaxed family evening, Jilly went to the window and drew back the curtains and looked out. The red setting sun was shining on the snow, making it glitter like rubies. In the shadowy hollows where the sun did not reach, the snow looked dark blue. Lady Harrington had been going to lend them jewels for the ball, real jewels, sapphires for Mandy, emeralds for Jilly. Lady Harrington had laughed as she had explained that young misses normally did not wear anything fancier than coral or pearls but that their very first ball was such an occasion, they should celebrate it with some glitter.

What were they doing, Lord Ranger and Lord Paul? Dances and parties were everyday events in their lives. A country hop was probably just another boring occasion they were glad to be free from. To her horror, she felt her eyes filling with tears and brushed them angrily away before turning around.

"It is the first really big disappointment we have had since coming here," said Mandy. "I had begun to think this a magic place where no matter what happened, everything would come right in the end. Now I am tortured with thoughts that Mrs. Tenby will hold her own impromptu dance and Lord Paul will dance with Lucinda and smile at Lucinda and . . . Oh, it is all past bearing!"

Colonel Tenby's party arrived at the ball. "Be glad when this is over," muttered Lord Paul as they went through the red-leather-covered doors and into the assembly rooms.

"Remember that it is the Davenport girls' first ball," replied Lord Ranger. "Let us make sure they enjoy themselves."

Both men looked around the room. "How odd!" exclaimed Lord Paul. "I would have sworn Lady Harrington would have been here with the girls before us. It was late when Mrs. Tenby decided to call a halt to that silly treasure hunt. I don't really believe there was any treasure to be found."

"Maybe Lady Harrington is teaching the Davenport girls how to make an entrance," remarked his friend.

"Lady Harrington is not like that, and neither are the Davenport girls. You do not think they have had an accident?"

"No, but I must admit I feel something is wrong." Lord Ranger strolled over to Mr. Nash. "What's happened to the Harrington party?" he asked.

"I do not know, my lords," said Mr. Nash. "They are bound to be here soon." He scuttled off and shortly afterwards could be seen talking to Mrs. Tenby and throwing anguished little looks in their direction.

"I'm going to the Harringtons'," said Lord Ranger suddenly.

Lord Paul looked relieved. "Coming with you. Let's not wait for them to get the carriage poled up again. Take horses and ride. Won't do our evening dress much good, but who cares? I confess it's going to be a deuced dull evening without the Misses Davenport."

Lucinda and Harriet watched them go. Then Harriet found what she privately damned as a country lout bowing before her and requesting the pleasure of the next dance. She was about to refuse, but she remembered with anguish that Mrs. Tenby had warned her that to refuse any gentleman would mean she would have to refuse them all, and so she accepted with very bad grace and therefore had the doubtful honor of being led into the first country dance by the local butcher.

"Now, who can that be?" asked Sir John, hearing the thudding at the door knocker. "Hope no one in the village is ill."

The parlor maid came in with Lord Ranger and Lord Paul hard on her heels. Both men stopped short in surprise at the sight of Mandy and Jilly in two of their oldest and as-yet-unconverted gowns, sitting by the fire, playing with the baby.

"Why aren't *you* at the ball?" asked Lord Ranger.

"What ball?" asked Lady Harrington. "That creature, Nash's servant, arrived late this afternoon with a message to say that the floor had fallen in with dry rot."

"Fustian!" said Lord Paul. "We have just left the assembly rooms, and the floor is perfect and the ball goes ahead. Have you got that letter from Nash? No, later, later. There has been some error. There is still time to get dressed."

"Come, girls," commanded Lady Harrington. Jilly and Mandy leapt to their feet. "Husband, dear, you are going to have to bustle into your evening clothes. We will not be long, my lords. In fact, our speed will amaze you." She swept out of the room with Jilly and Mandy.

So there was no leisurely, dreamy toilet. All the maids in the house rushed about to help. There were no elaborate hairstyles for them. Hair was pinned up on top of their heads, and Lady Harrington added tiaras of emeralds and sapphires to go with the necklaces she had promised them, and the final result was more dazzling than anything she could have hoped to achieve had they not had to rush.

Lord Ranger felt his heart lurch as Jilly walked into the room. Her eyes shone as bright as the emeralds round her neck and in her hair. The soft green muslin of her high-waisted gown appeared to have been molded to her body. Mandy was a delightful contrast in blue, but Lord Ranger only spared her a glance before his eyes went back to Jilly.

Lady Harrington's maid helped the girls into warm cloaks. Lord Ranger held out his arm to Jilly; Lord Paul, his to Mandy. Lady Harrington flashed a triumphant look at her husband. "Shall we go?" she said.

When Mrs. Tenby saw the party walking into the ballroom, her heart sank. The normally amiable Lady Harrington had a militant glint in her eye. A country dance was in progress. Mr. Nash, as master of ceremonies, was in front of the orchestra, calling out the figures of the dance—"Cross hands and down the middle"—and then his voice rose to a squeak as he saw the Harringtons' party.

That beautiful *famille verte* plate could go unclaimed. He was not going to stay and face Lady Harrington or Sir John. When the dance finished, he scuttled out by the back door and off into the night. Let Mrs. Tenby do any explaining. He was sure if he stayed hidden for a few days, then the Harringtons would forget all about it.

Lucinda and Harriet watched as Lord Ranger led Jilly to the floor for the next dance, which was the quadrille. Mandy was partnered by Lord Paul. There was no chance for them to compete. No one asked them to dance. Their haughty manners had frightened off the locals, and their pursuit of Lord Ranger and Lord Paul had made the other young men at the house party look elsewhere.

Lady Harrington went and sat down next to Mrs. Tenby. She opened her reticule and took out Mr. Nash's letter. "What was all this about, I wonder?" said Lady Harrington.

"Oh, about the floor. Tiresome man," said Mrs. Tenby. "First the ball was off, then on."

"I am determined to get to the bottom of this." Lady Harrington scanned the letter again and then put it back in her reticule. "I see Mr. Nash has escaped. I shall call on him tomorrow."

"He is a trifle eccentric, as you know." Mrs. Tenby began to feel frightened. Everything was changing. Her husband had gone off to the card room, a thing he would never have dreamed of doing before. It was all the fault of those wretched Davenport girls! She had to get to Mr. Nash before Lady Harrington did. For Lady Harrington had turned to the dowager on her other side and was describing the odd letter she had received about the ballroom floor, and the dowager was exclaiming in surprise and asking the lady next to *her*, and it was being borne in on Lady Harrington that, with the exception of Mrs. Tenby, who claimed to have had a similar letter, no one else had received one.

Although she often prided herself on having to

deal with all matters herself, Mrs. Tenby felt her husband ought to be by her side to help her, and then remembered in the next moment that he knew nothing about it, and then the moment after that, that the *famille verte* plate was his and that he was proud of it. For the first time in years, she felt weak and inclined to weep.

She muttered some excuse and then rose and went out of the ballroom. She looked this way and that. All the guests had arrived. The entrance hall was quiet. Mr. Nash lived in a large mansion a few yards behind the White Hart on the Oxford Road. She collected her cloak and swung it about her shoulders and made her way there, only remembering when she got outside that she was not wearing pattens and that she could feel the cold of the snow through her thin dancing pumps before she had gone a few steps. But worry made her ignore the discomfort. She would probably need to promise him that dish in order to make him lie low for a few days. Then . . . oh, then she would say it had been broken . . . or something.

Back in the ballroom the dancers were flying about the floor. Lord Ranger could not help thinking that the arrival of the Davenport girls had lightened the atmosphere. They enthusiastically accepted dances with everyone who asked them, and he thought cynically that most of the burghers of Moreton must be half in love with them already.

Manners prompted him to dance with Harriet, and then he found to his chagrin that it was the supper dance, so instead of taking Jilly in to her first ball supper, which he had been looking forward to immensely, he found he had to sit and talk flirtatious nonsense with Harriet. It was small consolation that Lord Paul had found himself similarly trapped with Lucinda. Mandy was partnered by that Jensen, and Jilly was laughing and talking to that young fool, Travers.

No one looking at the sparkling Davenport girls could realize that their every thought was concentrated on those two lords sitting so far away from them at the other end of one of the long tables.

Worse was to follow. For when the interminable supper dragged to an end, Lord Ranger and Lord Paul found that the girls' dance cards were full. It seemed only polite for them to dance once more with Harriet and Lucinda. The dance was the one waltz on the program. Jilly, being swung round in the arms of the baker, thought wistfully of all her dreams of dancing with Lord Ranger, and Mandy, being partnered again by Mr. Jensen, felt her smile becoming stiffer and stiffer with the effort to appear cheerful.

The ball finished at one o'clock. With sore feet and sore hearts, the Davenport girls were driven back to Greenbanks, where son James and his wife, Betty, were waiting up to ask them eager questions about how they had enjoyed it.

Mandy answered that it had all been so wonderful while privately thinking that when this holiday was over, when they had to go back to Yorkshire, the separation might actually come as a relief.

When they went upstairs and were undressed and made ready for bed, Jilly waited for Mandy to come through to have a chat about the ball, but Mandy was too cast down to want to talk about it. When Jilly finally went in to Mandy's bedroom, it was to find her sister apparently fast asleep.

* * *

A few miles away Lord Ranger was sitting on the end of his friend's bed. "The Davenport girls were enchanting tonight," he said.

"I am glad they are enjoying themselves so much," replied Lord Paul. "I had a talk with Sir John in the cardroom. He was quite incensed over their parents, Mr. and Mrs. Davenport. Seems the poor things have known nothing but strictness and beatings and corrections of one form or another. He was anxious I should not mention any of our conversation to his wife."

"Odso!"

"Yes, and you will not like the reason, either. Sir John is monstrous fond of the Davenport girls, but he is worried that his wife has become a little carried away. He says that Lady Harrington sees us both as prospective husbands and begs us to keep clear."

Lord Ranger thought with sudden anger of being barred from further enjoyable visits to Greenbanks. "We are always being seen in the light of husbands," he said.

"I think perhaps he was not just talking about his wife. He more or less implied that we are perhaps raising the hopes of two young, innocent girls, girls who must soon go back to their strict Puritan home."

"We have done nothing. We took Lady Harriet and Miss Lucinda in to supper, and no one thinks *that* means anything."

"In the case of Lucinda and Harriet, neither I, you, nor anyone else cares what they think. They have both been out, both are accomplished flirts, and both are as hard as steel. Not only did they ruin the Davenports' ball gowns, but I think they were behind some ruse to try to get Mr. Nash to stop the Harrington party attending the ball. But I can see the sense in what Sir John was trying to tell me . . . to tell us."

Lord Ranger scowled. "So does that apply to Travers and Jensen?"

"Travers and Jensen are capable of being every bit as happy with either Miss Charteris or Miss Andrews."

"Do you think either of the Davenport girls regard us in the light of future husbands?"

"No, I don't," said Lord Paul candidly. "But I am become fond of Sir John and I think the gentlemanly thing to do would be to keep away."

"It is so dull here." Lord Ranger sighed. "What do you say? Do we make our adieux and head back to London?"

Lord Paul's black eyes held an unreadable expression. Then he said, "Perhaps after Christmas. Sir John cannot object us to calling during the Christmas festivities. I would like to see how Miss Mandy . . . I mean, how both of them enjoy their first, and probably their last Christmas."

But it was before Christmas when Jilly and Mandy saw them again. Jilly and Mandy were helping with the festivities for Saint Thomas's Day on the twenty-first of December. Mandy appeared more settled and happier now that there was no Lord Paul around to disturb her, but in Jilly's case, absence had made the heart grow fonder and she sometimes told herself gloomily that while her sister was recovering from love, she herself was falling into it.

Saint Thomas was the patron saint of old people,

so this was the day for giving them small presents of money to help them buy their Christmas food. The poor children of the parish also went around on Saint Thomas's Day to ask for corn for their frumenty cakes, or sweets. Frumenty was a kind of porridge made from grains of wheat boiled in milk and then seasoned with sugar and cinnamon. After the special bags the children carried to put the corn in, it was called "going a-corning." As they toured the village, they sang:

"Christmas is coming and the geese are getting fat,
Please spare a penny for the old man's hat,
If you haven't got a penny, a ha'penny will do,
If you haven't got a ha'penny, God bless you."

Also on Saint Thomas's Day was wassailing, and after Jilly and Mandy had helped to distribute money to the old folk, they joined the singers who went from house to house with the wassail bowl, decorated with ribbons, garlands, and a gilded apple.

Wassail is in fact a centuries-old toast. Like Father Christmas, mistletoe, and the mummers' plays, it was a tradition that the church did not try to stop. The word comes from the Anglo-Saxon *wes hal*, meaning "be whole." It was customary for every family to have a wassailing bowl steaming away throughout the Christmas season. The traditional content of the wassail bowl was "lamb's wool," which was made by mixing hot ale with the pulp of roasted apples and adding sugar and spices. The full recipe went: "Boil three pints of ale; beat six eggs, the whites and yokes together; set both to the fire in a pewter pot; add roasted apples, sugar, beaten nutmegs, cloves, and ginger; and being well brewed, drink it while hot."

The snow had melted since the night of the ball, and the remaining slush had frozen hard into long bluish white ridges which lay across the fields like the long fingers of winter. The sky was leaden when the girls went round the village with the wassail bowl. Jilly and Mandy were beginning to feel quite tipsy, for they and the other revelers helped themselves to a small tankard of the contents at each house. Both girls were crowned with garlands of holly and had a multitude of colored ribbons tied in bows on their gowns and tied into the fur edging of their cloaks.

They had given up watching for two mounted figures and so it came as a surprise when they looked up and saw Lord Ranger and Lord Paul, both on horseback, watching them.

Lady Harrington cried, "Welcome! We are just finished. Will you join us at the house? Sir John will give you something hot to drink, for this bowl is nigh empty."

The men raised their hats and rode on. Lord Ranger was startled at the effect the sight of Jilly had had on him; Jilly like some pagan goddess with the holly wreath in her red hair.

With a feeling of coming home, both men entered Greenbanks. The maid ushered them into the drawing room and there was Sir John, mixing punch with all the single-minded concentration of a good child.

"Sit down, gentlemen," he cried when the little maid tugged at his sleeve to attract his attention.

"You must have some of my special mixture to banish the cold."

Lord Ranger experienced an odd feeling of anticipation and excitement such as he had not had since a child. He and Lord Paul had stayed away from Greenbanks, and Mrs. Tenby had been assiduous in providing amusements to distract them. But the Christmas spirit had not yet come to the colonel's, and Lord Ranger was sure it never would. Peter, the footman, had been heard asking if he should get the staff to decorate the rooms with holly and ivy, and Mrs. Tenby had said she did not want to risk any damage to walls or ornaments with that "filthy stuff."

There were piles of the "filthy stuff," ready-cut and lying just outside the front door. Lord Ranger was sure the Harringtons meant to throw themselves heart and soul into Christmas.

Jilly and Mandy came in, cheeks pink with the cold, laughing and saying they must get the holly wreaths out of their hair. "Why?" asked Lord Ranger. "They look most charming."

Both men had stood up at the girls' entrance. The colonel cried, "Punch, everyone. This is my best yet."

"I think we have had enough to drink already," laughed Jilly. "No, Mandy, you must not have any more."

"I shall do very well," said Mandy. "The fresh air has cleared my head."

But she stumbled as she passed Lord Paul, and would have fallen had he not grabbed her around the waist to support her. For one brief, delirious moment she leaned against him, her head bowed submissively. For one brief moment he felt those young breasts pressed against him, smelled the scent of her hair, felt the sudden quickening of his senses. And then she had detached herself and with a nervous little laugh, turned to her sister. "Come with me, Jilly. This holly prickles so."

The girls went upstairs together. "Steady," admonished Jilly.

Mandy shook her head in bewilderment. "I thought I was getting over it," she said. "I thought of him a lot, but I began to feel more at ease with myself, just grateful that I had met him, that I had the memory of him to take home. Now that I see him again, all those awful burning, yearning feelings have started up again. Of course, you don't know what I mean, sis. How could you?"

Jilly turned away and began to lift the holly wreath from her hair. "No," she lied, "I don't know what you mean. But both gentlemen have been extremely kind to us, so we must be as cheerful as possible. The best you can hope for, Mandy, is to leave *him* with a bright memory of *you*. So we will laugh and be cheerful, shall we not?"

"Yes." Mandy sat down on the bed. "Yes. I will be better if I have a role to play. But do you think we can have them to ourselves for a little or will that precious pair, Lucinda and Harriet, ride over, do you think?"

"Perhaps. But if they do, we shall behave with dignity."

"There is no moon tonight," said Mandy. "Although it is but a short distance from here to the colonel's, I don't think they will venture out."

Chapter Six

"*T*HAT IS THE Harringtons' boy," said Harriet, looking out of the window, "and our gentlemen are gone from the house. Do not tell me they are back at Greenbanks!"

"It all points to that," remarked Lucinda crossly. "What do we do now? Set off in pursuit?"

"We must be a bit more subtle than that." Harriet sat for a while in thought. "Mrs. Tenby has proved a clumsy ally. Besides, she is too taken up with her husband at the moment, who is showing every sign of avoiding her at all times. She has been fretting and asking where he is. I know where he is, for I saw him setting off with his guns and his dogs. The servants are loyal to him and won't tell her, something she does not seem to have realized."

"I have it." Lucinda brightened. "We shall tell her that the colonel has ridden to Greenbanks. We shall be sympathetic. We shall offer to accompany her."

Harriet laughed. "Let's go and do it now."

They found Mrs. Tenby in the Yellow Saloon. Harriet was just wondering how to raise the subject when Mrs. Tenby said fretfully as soon as she saw them, "I do not know what has happened to the colonel. How many of us are there going to be for dinner? It is most inconsiderate of him. Your lords are gone to Greenbanks, I regret to say," she added with a certain amount of satisfaction at spreading the misery around.

"And that is where Colonel Tenby is," said Harriet lightly.

Mrs. Tenby looked startled and then furious. She had had to hand that valuable plate over to Mr. Nash, she had had to tell her furious husband that she had broken it. But Mr. Nash had lain low by going off to Oxford to stay with friends, and so Lady Harrington, when she called, had not been able to find out anything.

"He had no *right* to go to Greenbanks without telling me," snapped Mrs. Tenby. "I shall go there directly."

"We will accompany you, if you like," said Harriet.

"No need. I am quite capable of going on my own, thank you very much."

"With us, you would appear less the outraged wife," said Harriet in a cool voice. "It would look more like a party and less like a warring raid."

Mrs. Tenby opened her mouth to berate her for impertinence and then suddenly saw the force of the argument. "Very well," she said. "But I have no intention of telling the kitchens we shall be absent for dinner. A brief call should suffice."

To her surprise, Harriet and Lucinda, who were notorious for taking a long time to dress, were ready in under half an hour. As the carriage bowled down the drive, Harriet, looking out of the window in the failing light, saw the colonel strolling back with his gun under his arm and his dog at his heels. She quickly seized the red leather curtains and drew them close. "Such a dismal prospect," she said lightly.

Lady Harrington was delighted with Mandy and Jilly. They were in sparkling good form, encouraging Lord Paul to give them all the London gossip, and laughing with delight at his sometimes wicked stories. The punch circulated, the fire crackled, and Lady Harrington smiled on them all and said that perhaps they should start to decorate the house. It was somehow accepted that the two lords should stay for dinner.

Lord Ranger was hanging holly on the picture frame above the fireplace, looking down at Jilly and saying that she looked like a piece of holly herself with her red hair and green eyes, and Mandy was sitting on the floor wreathing colored ribbons among fir boughs, when the maid entered and said, "Please my lady, Mrs. Tenby and party."

"Rats," said Lady Harrington inelegantly. "And just when we were having fun. Show them in."

Lucinda and Harriet stood in the doorway and surveyed the scene: Lord Ranger and Jilly standing with bunches of holly in their hands, Mandy and Lord Paul sitting unceremoniously on the floor with fir boughs in front of them. The bright room smelled of rum punch and evergreens.

Despite their hurried dressing, Lucinda and Harriet looked as if they had stepped out of a fashion plate in *La Belle Assemblée*. Jilly and Mandy immediately became aware that they were still in their Saint Thomas's Day fancy dress embellished with gaudy ribbons.

Immediately everything became formal. James and Betty scooped up their beloved baby and left the room. Mandy got up and sat down on a chair and smoothed down her skirt with nervous hands.

"I understood my husband was here," said Mrs. Tenby, looking around.

"No, we have not seen the colonel," said Sir John, "and more's the pity. He is very good company."

Mrs. Tenby looked nonplussed and then threw a sudden sharp look at Lucinda and Harriet, who gazed limpidly back.

Lady Harrington caught that exchange and interpreted it correctly. Harriet and Lucinda had told Mrs. Tenby that the colonel was to be found at Greenbanks so as to give themselves an excuse to call.

But Mrs. Tenby was jealous of Lady Harrington, for had not her husband obviously preferred her hospitality to that of his own wife? And so she was all at once determined to stay. Lady Harrington should not snatch these two matrimonial prizes from under her nose.

The relaxed atmosphere had left the room. Lady Harrington asked the maids to take out the decorations; they would finish them on the following day. Lord Ranger and Lord Paul were annoyed with Mrs. Tenby and paid particular attention to Mandy and Jilly. That was, until Sir John gently drew Lord Paul aside and said, "I hope you are going to heed my advice." Lady Harrington's sharp eyes noticed the exchange, and she wondered what her husband had said to bring that dark look to Lord Paul's eyes. Then she marked the way that Lord Paul in turn drew Lord Ranger aside and the look of displeasure on Lord Ranger's face.

It was borne in on Lady Harrington as she noticed the way the two gentlemen promptly turned their attentions to Lucinda and Harriet that her normally indolent husband had warned them off.

But try as Lady Harrington would to get a word alone with her husband for the rest of that dreadful evening, he seemed to escape her, and so she had to sit and fume, watching the sadness grow in Jilly and Mandy's eyes, observing how Lucinda and Harriet were glowing in a vulgar triumphant sort of way, which unfortunately added considerably to their beauty.

She had to ask the Tenby party to stay for dinner, and hospitable though she normally was, Lady Harrington found herself becoming resentful. It had been such a jolly, pleasant day, a day in which she had been able to forget that "her" two charming girls were not a permanent fixture, that the day would come when they had to return home to a very bleak life indeed.

"Have you heard from your parents?" she suddenly heard Mrs. Tenby ask the Davenport girls.

Lady Harrington flinched. She had received several letters, some addressed to her, some addressed to Jilly and Mandy. She had opened and read them all but had not passed them on to the girls. They were full of such depressing admonitions.

"No," said Jilly, "and I hope all is well. I put in our letters that we had not heard a word, but Lady Harrington made me take that bit out, for she said it would worry Mama and Papa unnecessarily."

Lady Harrington saw the sharp look in Mrs. Tenby's eyes. "How odd," said that lady, "for my husband received a letter only the other day from friends in Yorkshire."

"Yes, very odd." Lady Harrington signaled to one of the maids. "Bring in the pudding, Mary."

Lady Harrington was now seriously worried. She would need to tell the girls about those letters, should have done so before. But, she consoled herself, there was still plenty of time. The roads between the Cotswolds and Yorkshire would be too bad until the spring to allow Mr. and Mrs. Davenport to travel.

Normally they would all have retired to the drawing room and danced or played games, but Lady Harrington became as chilly a hostess as Mrs. Tenby and urged Lucinda to play the piano and Harriet to sing because that kept them from ogling and flirting.

At eleven o'clock Lady Harrington said firmly that she was extremely fatigued. It had been a long day. She remained standing until Lord Ranger and Lord Paul got to their feet, until Mrs. Tenby said they should be going home, until Harriet and Lucinda had been helped into their cloaks.

Lady Harrington noticed uneasily that Lucinda flashed a triumphant sort of I-know-something-you-don't-know look in the Davenport girls' direction and wondered what she had been plotting.

Lord Ranger and Lord Paul made very stately and formal good-byes. Jilly smiled and waved, but she put a protective arm around her sister's waist and her eyes were sad.

When the party had disappeared into the night, Lady Harrington, her face grim, turned to her husband. "You cannot escape me now. A word with you in private."

* * *

"That went very well," said Harriet with satisfaction when she and Lucinda were alone again. "Did you mark those silly gowns they had on? Like peasant girls. And what do you think of what Mrs. Tenby said on the road home, that she believed that Lady Harrington had not been showing any letters from the Davenports to their daughters?"

Lucinda giggled. "I have been saving a great surprise for you. You will never guess how wicked I have been."

"Surprise me."

"After that first skating party, I felt something had to be done."

"We discussed that."

"No, no, it is something else. I asked Colonel Tenby if he knew where the Davenports lived, and he said as a matter of fact he did—Marston Park, outside Darlington." Lucinda hugged herself in glee. "This is the best bit. I wrote to Mrs. Davenport and sent it express."

"You *what*!"

"I wrote to Mrs. Davenport. I said I shared her sympathies about Christmas, for it is well-known that the Davenports are famous Puritans. I said it was sad that the Harringtons should be introducing Miss Jilly and Miss Mandy—silly names—to such wicked frivolity such as skating parties with well-known rakes, not to mention encouraging them to look forward to and take part in every pagan ritual of Christmas."

Harriet looked at her in horror. "But they will post south to rescue their daughters from sin as soon as possible. If letters can get through, and they evidently can, they will be here quite soon. Do you know that the new mail coaches can travel from

London to Edinburgh in thirty-four and half hours? It will take less than that from York."

"Pooh! That was the whole idea in writing to them."

"But they will produce your letter. You will be exposed as a sneak."

"Not I. I am not so silly. I used a plain seal and scrawled some indecipherable signature at the bottom of the page."

A slow smile dawned on Harriet's face. "You clever puss. They should be here any day now."

"Yes, because although we have had some snow here, it has nearly cleared, and Colonel Tenby's friend who wrote to him from Yorkshire said they had had no snow there yet at all, an exceptionally mild winter in the North."

Harriet said, "It is cold again and the sky is leaden. What if it should snow and block the roads before they arrive?"

"I am sure they are nearly here. Besides, these northern Puritans are a hardy lot. To save their chicks from evil, they are quite capable of walking!"

And both began to laugh.

"It is not like you to interfere," Lady Harrington was saying to her chastened husband. "Rakes, indeed. Those gentlemen have been the soul of kindness to my chicks."

"Not your chicks."

"I feel as close to them as if they were my own daughters. They would be a steadying influence. They are ideally suited. Things were going splendidly until you interfered. They had eyes only for Jilly and Mandy until you put your oar in."

"Well, my dear, it is not like you to be so cross with me," pleaded Sir John. "I thought I was doing it for the best. But only think. The Davenports are good blood, but not equal to a duke's family. They could be, but their very parsimoniousness and Puritanism put them beyond the pale."

"Now I don't know how to lure them back," fretted his wife, hardly listening to him. "Christmas at Mrs. Tenby's will be such a dismal affair that I am sure the young people at least will call, and perhaps our lords with them."

Upstairs, Jilly was trying to cheer Mandy by reading to her from a book of Richard Steele's essays. "Only hear this, Mandy," she said, and began to read aloud:

"I am a young woman and have my fortune to make, for which reason I come constantly to Church to hear Divine Service, and make Conquests; but one great Hindrance in this my design is that our Clerk, who was once a Gardener, has this Christmas so over-decked the Church with Greens that he has quite spoiled my prospect, insomuch that I have scarce seen the young Baronet I dress at these last three Weeks, though we both have been very Constant at our Devotions, and do not sit above three Pews off. The Church, as it is now equipped, looks more like a Greenhouse than a Place of Worship; in the middle Isle is a very pretty Shady Walk, and the Pews look like so many Arbours on each side of it. The Pulpit itself has such Clusters of Ivy, Holly and Rosemary about it that a light Fellow in our Pew took Occasion to say that The Congregation heard the Word out of a Bush, like Moses."

Mandy gave a rueful little laugh. "No one could accuse us of having *dressed* at our lords tonight. What guys we looked in our fancy dress compared to Lucinda and Harriet."

Jilly frowned. "I think it is all most odd. Our gentlemen were paying every attention to us and then suddenly they grew cool and talked to Lucinda and Harriet as if they were the only ladies in the room. I felt diminished and very unfashionable and shabby."

The door opened and Lady Harrington came in. "Good, you are still awake. I have a confession to make." She told them about the letters from home, ending up by saying ruefully, "It was indeed very bad of me. I have kept them all, but for the first, which I regret to say I burned. Here they are. I should not judge what you should read or not read."

So after she had gone, Jilly and Mandy read the letters, feeling the iron fetters of rigid behavior closing about them.

"I refuse to worry," said Jilly at last. "It is not as if they will come all the way south to get us in the middle of winter. They will arrive in the spring, and Christmas will be long past, and I am sure Lady Harrington will not tell them about the celebrations. Mandy, we should put these two gentlemen right out of our heads. They are not for us, and sighing and dreaming about them is only going to spoil everything for us."

"So you, too?" asked Mandy in a little voice.

"Yes, I, too. So we will stick together and see it through and have as much fun as we can."

Mr. Travers, Mr. Andrews, Belinda, and Margaret arrived the next day when they were hard at work with the decorations.

The tradition of bringing holly and ivy and mistletoe or any other evergreen into the house was a Christmas practice that went back to the Romans. Bringing evergreens home and presenting branches to people was a custom in Rome during the Christmas celebrations; evergreen was a token of good luck. It was relatively easy for the church to make holly a Christian symbol. Its sharp leaves and red berries became associated with Christ's crown of thorns. Ivy was more difficult, it being associated with Bacchus, the Roman god of wine. Nevertheless, the customs and superstitions associated with holly and ivy, like the Yule log, had really nothing to do with Christianity at all.

Lady Harrington told them that in the Cotswolds the tradition was that if the first holly to be brought into the house was prickly, the master would rule for the coming year; if the holly was smooth-leaved, then the mistress would rule. Sir John said ruefully that it did not matter whether the holly brought into Greenbanks was prickly or plain, for Lady Harrington *always* ruled the roost.

With many sly looks at the ladies, Mr. Travers asked if there was to be a mistletoe bough. Sir John grinned and said they always had one over the door. "Though the church don't approve," he added.

"They do at York Minster," explained Mandy shyly. "It is the only church in the whole of Britain exempt from the rule that mistletoe is not to be used as a church decoration. Each Christmas a bough of mistletoe is brought in by the clergy and laid on the altar, and then they proclaim ... How does it go, Jilly?"

"They proclaim 'a public liberty, pardon, and freedom to all sorts of inferior and even wicked people at the gates of the city to the four corners of the earth.' "

"Forgiveness for all, hey?" said Mr. Jensen. "I like that."

"At our seminary," put in Belinda, "we were told that mistletoe was pagan because it was a custom of the Druids. The arch Druid was supposed to have cut the mistletoe with a golden sickle during November each year. It was caught as it fell from the tree by virgins holding out a white cloth. This was followed by a prayer and the sacrifice of white oxen. The mistletoe was then divided up amongst the people, who took it home to hang over their doors. It was held to work miracles of healing, to protect against witchcraft, and to bring fertility to the land and the people of the house." She blushed suddenly as if she had caught herself out in saying something indecent.

"Well, we just put it over the door," said Sir John cheerfully, "and Jimmy brings it. No virgins or gold sickles necessary. Then each time you gentlemen kiss one of the ladies, you pluck off a berry, and when all the berries are gone, no more kissing."

How quickly one became used to freedom, thought Jilly sadly. Just after their arrival, she and Mandy would have been thrilled by all the fun and chatter, and yet both of them stiffened every time they heard a horseman out on the road. And could they really return to the life they had once led? But rebellion was not possible. Their parents held the purse strings.

They had even lost the attention of Mr. Travers and Mr. Jensen, who seemed happy with Belinda and Margaret. They might even propose, thought Jilly enviously, and their parents would be delighted and no obstacle would be put in their way.

But one look at Mandy's wistful face rallied her. She would not let anything spoil their day.

She had not counted on the arrival of Colonel Tenby.

The colonel was seriously worried. He had had an acrimonious exchange with his wife the night before, and for once, he had got the better of her. He had stated firmly that she had to change her ways. He was unhappy. He felt quite amazed at his courage when he thought again of the way he had stood up to her. But it was when he had been retiring to his room, which was along the corridor from those occupied by Lucinda and Harriet, that he had heard the girls laughing and then he distinctly heard Harriet say, "You are indeed wicked, Lucinda. When the Davenports get that letter you wrote to them, they will scorch the earth beneath their chariot wheels racing to rescue their daughters from corruption."

He had stood appalled, debating whether to enter the room and demand to know why they had done such a terrible thing. But he knew at the same moment that they would both deny it, say he had misheard and be politely shocked that he should do such an ungentlemanly thing as to listen at doors.

He felt he could not turn to his wife. He had noticed Mrs. Tenby's machinations to make a match between Lord Ranger, Lord Paul, and Harriet and

Lucinda. He realized his wife would think what Lucinda had done was fair game and then she would no doubt help her in her lies that no such letter had been sent. It was then he thought of Lady Harrington and decided to ride over to Greenbanks.

The air was very quiet and still and his horse's hooves rang on the iron of the frost-bound road. Snow to come, he thought, looking up at the sky. The countryside seemed to be waiting for it. Nothing moved in the quiet gray landscape, and even the smoke from cottage chimneys hung in long, thin columns on the bitter air.

When he arrived at Greenbanks, Jimmy was hoisting the mistletoe bough over the door and Mr. Travers was already kissing all the ladies while Sir John laughed and plucked off berries for each kiss until Lady Harrington cried on Mr. Travers to stop or there would be no berries left for anyone else, meaning no kisses.

Jilly and Mandy were disappointed in their first kisses. Mr. Travers's mouth had been a trifle wet, and both were hard put to stop themselves from taking out their handkerchiefs and scrubbing their mouths.

Then they both heard the clip-clop of a horse's hooves out on the road, coming ever nearer to the gate at the end of the short drive. Jilly could see hope springing up in Mandy's eyes. One horse, thought Jilly. They would surely come together if they were coming at all.

And then her hopes were dashed when Sir John cried, "Here comes the colonel, and looking deuced grim, too. I wonder what the matter is."

Jimmy ran to take the colonel's horse as he swung down from the saddle. "Good day," said the colonel. "Sir John and Lady Harrington, an urgent word with you in private, if you please."

Wondering, they led him indoors to a small morning room. "Now, Colonel," said Sir John. "Sit down and tell us what ails you. For you are looking like Winter himself."

"This has been the last straw," said the colonel wearily, passing his hand over his brow and slightly dislodging his white wig. "I was on my way to bed last night when I overheard Harriet and Lucinda talking. As far as I can gather, Lucinda has sent a letter to Mr. and Mrs. Davenport warning them that their daughters are being led astray."

"And what did they say to that when you confronted them?"

"I did not. I did not know what to do. I was sure Lucinda would simply lie and say I had misheard. You can guess how they would go about it. People who listen at doors never hear the right thing. That sort of business. A gentlemen *never* listens at doors. This has been a dreadful holiday. My wife . . . my wife has somehow got it into her head that she can marry off Lucinda and Harriet to Lord Paul and Lord Ranger, and they . . . they are using her for their own ends. Demme, I wish I had never left my regiment. You know what they'll be doing at the barracks at Christmas? There'll be fun and balls and parties. Look at me. I am an old man."

"Nonsense," said Sir John hurriedly. "Same age as myself."

"I feel like a hundred," said the colonel fretfully. "Do you know, I am not going to put up with this one moment longer. I am going back to my regiment and I am leaving today! Because if I wait much longer, the snow I fear is coming will begin to fall and block the roads. For your sakes, I hope it does. For if those Davenports arrive, the first sight of an evergreen branch will have them hauling their daughters off, no matter what the weather."

"Perhaps the Davenports never received that letter," said Lady Harrington hopefully. "I mean the last letter arrived here not so long ago, and it was full of ranting and raving about Christmas but not a word about having received any letter."

"What should I do about Lucinda?" asked the colonel.

"Nothing," said Lady Harrington sweetly. "*I* will attend to the matter." She turned to her husband. "You entertain our young guests. I will take the carriage and go back with the colonel. I am afraid, Colonel, that I am also going to give your wife a piece of my mind. It is my belief she coerced Mr. Nash into writing a letter to me telling me the ball at Moreton was canceled. Mr. Nash has disappeared, but he cannot hide forever, and I will get the truth out of him sooner or later."

"I don't care," said the colonel. "I'm going home to pack!"

Mr. and Mrs. Davenport and the maid, Abigail, had left the mail coach and transferred to the Oxford coach. They had not noticed the rigors of the journey. Mortification was good for the soul. Both were fired with crusading zeal. They had not sent any warning of their impending arrival. The Harringtons must be given no time to take down those pagan decorations, the Davenports naively assuming that the Harringtons would wish to cover up the evidence of their sin if forewarned. Even the last letter sent from the North had been left for a servant to post so that the Harringtons would not know they were already on the road.

The Davenports were not sad or worried, but angry and elated at the same time. The devil lurked around every corner, and it was their duty to thrash him out of hiding.

Lord Ranger and Lord Paul were playing billiards. "Have you noticed," asked Lord Ranger, "that the nearer Christmas draws, the more stultified the atmosphere in this house becomes? I suppose we ought to join the ladies, but Harriet will promptly produce her folio of dreadful watercolors for me to admire, and Lucinda, I believe, is netting you a purse."

"I just remembered. Gully Parker—do you remember old Gully, sold out when we did?—has a tidy place over near Chipping Norton. If we ride there today, we could have some fun now that the Harringtons are out of bounds."

"I don't care if the Harringtons are out of bounds, I am going there on Christmas day. I want to see those two young ladies enjoy their first Christmas, and nothing is gong to stop me," said Lord Ranger.

"Then let us go and join the ladies in the drawing room and break the news to Mrs. Tenby that she must live without us for the rest of the day and then we'll go and see Gully."

"Looks like snow. What if we get trapped?"

"Then we won't have to spend Christmas in this mausoleum. Come along."

They put on their coats and made their way upstairs to the drawing room.

At the sight of them, Harriet promptly struck

an Attitude. It was very fashionable for ladies to strike Attitudes, usually supposed to represent some heroine of Greek mythology. Harriet was meant to look like Pandora opening the box. She stared down at her work basket with an expression of horror on her face.

"Got indigestion, have you?" asked Lord Ranger. "It was that buttered crab at dinner the other night."

"Lady Harrington," announced Peter, the footman.

Lady Harrington, like a warship under full sail, walked into the room, followed by the colonel.

"My dear Lady Harrington," cried Mrs. Tenby. "To what do we owe the honor of this visit?"

Lady Harrington's bright eyes fastened on Lucinda. "You," she said in tones of loathing, "are a snake in the grass."

Lucinda stood up. "What can you mean, my lady?"

"I mean that you wrote to Mr. and Mrs. Davenport and told them that their daughters were celebrating Christmas, knowing full well that Christmas is anathema to those Puritans."

"That's a lie," shrieked Lucinda, turning pale.

"No, it's not," said the colonel. He caught sight of himself in the mirror and straightened his wig. "Heard you myself last night, you and Lady Harriet; laughing and chattering about it, you were."

"People who listen at doors never hear the right thing," said Harriet.

"Not with a precious pair like you," said Lady Harrington wrathfully. "And you . . ." She rounded on Mrs. Tenby. "I *know* you persuaded that sniveling creature, Nash, to write to me and tell me the ball at Moreton had been canceled. What did you bribe him with, hey? He has money enough."

"He is greedy for fine porcelain," said the colonel. "By God, madam, if I find out that is where my plate went and that it has not been broken, then I will wring Nash's scrawny neck."

"Because of your spite," went on Lady Harrington, glaring at Harriet and Lucinda, "the happiness of the Davenport girls is about to be destroyed sooner than it would have been. You have everything and yet you could not allow them a few simple pleasures without trying to ruin them. And that goes for you, too, Mrs. Tenby. Do not come near my house again."

"And get out of mine," shouted Mrs. Tenby with the boiling rage that sharp guilt can give the arrogant.

"This is *my* home," interrupted the colonel. "And when I am in residence, the Harringtons will always be welcome. But I have had enough. Now I am going to pack. I am going back to my regiment."

Lady Harrington saw the suddenly bewildered and lost look on Mrs. Tenby's face and felt a reluctant pang of sympathy.

"Good day to you all," she said, and turning on her heel, she left the room, and left a stricken silence behind her.

Chapter Seven

THE GIRLS WERE busy in the kitchens with Lady Harrington on Christmas eve while Sir John went out with the men from the village to supervise the dragging home of the Yule log.

Lady Harrington said she always baked the mince pie herself. Her recipe required these ingredients: one pheasant, one hare, one capon, two pigeons, and two rabbits. The meat was separated from the bone and minced into a fine hash. The livers and hearts of all these birds and animals were added along with two sheep's kidneys, little meat balls of beef and eggs and pickled mushrooms, salt, pepper, vinegar, and various spices, and the broth in which the bones were cooked. All this was ladled into a large piecrust and baked.

It was the custom, explained Lady Harrington as she worked busily away, to make a wish on the first bite of a mince pie. Perhaps the most famous of all Christmas pies, she said, was the one into which Jack Horner stuck his thumb:

> "Little Jack Horner
> Sat in a corner
> Eating his Christmas pie;
> He put in his thumb,

And pulled out a plum
And said what a good boy am I."

Begged to tell the story, she said the rhyme described how Jack Horner, a steward to Richard Whiting, the last abbot of Glastonbury, was sent to London at the time of the dissolution of the monasteries with a large Christmas pie as a gift for Henry VIII. Under the pastry were the title deeds to twelve manors belonging to the monastery, the abbot hoping to curry favor with the king. On the journey up to London, Jack Horner is said to have discovered the secret of the pie, and extracted for himself the title deeds to the manor of Mells in Somerset, where he went to live after the dissolution of Glastonbury.

"Is it not strange that a great number of so-called nursery rhymes were actually political satire?" said Jilly. "But in a world where children grow old and wizened before their time, it is not at all odd, I suppose."

To distract her mind from gloomy thoughts, Lady Harrington said, "We have an amusing local tradition. Have you heard of dumb cakes?"

"Now, what on earth is a dumb cake?" asked Mandy.

"Oh, it is for young girls who want to know who is going to marry them." At that moment Sir John walked into the kitchen and sat down at the scrubbed table. How easy and friendly the Harringtons were, thought Jilly for about the hundredth time. In what other household would the master sit easily in his kitchens with the servants?

"I was just telling them about dumb cakes, my dear," said Lady Harrington. "The girls have to make the cakes in absolute silence. Then they put the cakes in the oven and open the kitchen door. Their future husbands are supposed to walk in at midnight and turn the cake. Here, the girl puts her initials on the cake, and the future husband is supposed to take a sharp knife and prick his initials next to hers. Why do you not do it this evening?"

"Who will come?" asked Mandy, a shadow in her eyes.

"Probably no one," said Lady Harrington comfortably. "But you should make them just the same. Remember, Christmas is a magical time. You take an eggshell full of salt, another of wheatmeal, and a third of barley."

Mandy wrinkled her nose. "It does not sound very nice."

Lady Harrington laughed. "It is all fun. I have never seen anyone actually eat one of the things."

Jilly and Mandy almost forgot their sore hearts as the bustle went on about them in the kitchens while they helped the cook and the maids to chop vegetables and roll pastry.

Suspended from the ceiling on a hook was an enormous Norfolk turkey. Although turkeys had first been introduced from New England, they got their name from the merchants from the Levant or Turkey who brought them over. By the end of the eighteenth century Norwich alone was sending a thousand turkeys a day up to London. Charles Lamb, the great essayist, wrote to a friend who was spending the Christmas of 1815 in China, "You have no turkeys; you would not desecrate the festival by offering up a withered Chinese bantam instead of the savoury grand Norfolcian holocaust that smokes all around my nostrils at this moment from a thousand firesides."

But turkey was still only to be found on the tables of the comfortably off, the poorer contenting themselves with goose or capon.

On a dresser under the window was the Christmas pudding maturing away in its bowl.

Then Lady Harrington, having seen her pie tenderly placed in one of the ovens, suggested it was time for them to change and go to church.

Jilly and Mandy wished they could attend a church like the one at Benham St. Anne's when they got home. It was so jolly and friendly with everyone calling out "Happy Christmas" across the fir-bedecked aisles, and the pulpit was gay with shiny green holly with scarlet berries. The squire, Sir William Black, and his family came back with them after church, and the schoolteacher came and the vicar and the curate, all to share Sir John's punch or a tankard filled from the wassail bowl. The day gathered pace, full of noise and music. The waits came round to sing Christmas carols at the open door. Feathery flakes of snow were beginning to fall, and it was all so beautiful that Jilly felt tears rising to her eyes.

Then there were the presents to wrap and place on a table beside the tree.

Oh, that tree! The girls thought they would never forget the wonder of it when James Harrington lit the thin taper candles on the wide green branches while Sir John extinguished the lamps in the drawing room and snuffed the candles so that there was only the tree, shining and splendid in the darkness.

More people from the village began to arrive, for the Harringtons kept open house on Christmas eve, and the girls and Lady Harrington helped the maids by running here and there with trays of sandwiches, sugar plums, and cakes. Before the last guests left at eleven to trudge out through the shining, fluttering, whirling snow, the wassail bowl had had to be refilled several times and the Yule log dragged forward several more inches into the heart of the fire.

For a moment Jilly and Mandy stood side by side with Sir John and Lady Harrington, waving goodbye and shouting "Happy Christmas" and yet trying not to hope too fiercely to see two gentlemen riding up on horseback. Lady Harrington had told them that Jimmy had found out that Lord Ranger and Lord Paul had gone to stay with a friend at Chipping Norton.

Surely they would return to the Tenbys' for Christmas day, thought Jilly, and surely they would drop in, if only to say Happy Christmas.

But one by one the twinkling lamps of the guests vanished into the night and left only darkness and swirling snow.

Lady Harrington gave a little sigh as if she, too, was disappointed.

But she turned to the girls and said, "Off to the kitchens with you and bake those cakes. Cook has left the recipe and instructions on the kitchen table."

When the girls had gone she walked back into the drawing room with her husband and picked up the candle snuffer and began to extinguish the lights on the Christmas tree one by one while her husband lit the lamps.

"Did you tell them about Lucinda writing to their parents?" asked Sir John.

"Not yet. Why ruin Christmas by seeing the fear in their eyes or watching them cringe every time they hear a carriage on the road? Boxing Day. I will tell them on Boxing Day. If there were any way I could legally adopt those girls, then I would, but can you imagine the battle in the courts? It would be such a scandal."

She went to the window and drew back the curtains and looked out at the falling snow. "I keep praying for a miracle," she said. "They will soon go out of our lives and we shall never see or hear from them again. They will each be married off to grim Puritans and grow old before their time."

"Everyone should have good memories," said Sir John. "You have given them Christmas and they will never forget it. Good memories make one brave. They will be stronger in spirit because of it."

Down in the kitchens, Jilly and Mandy were taking turns to stir the mixture in the bowl. "I hope this is all right," said Jilly, peering at the unappetizing-looking mixture.

"It doesn't matter," said Mandy. "No one's going to eat the things. Are we going to open the kitchen door at midnight?"

"Why not?" said Jilly. "It's all part of the tradition. As soon as midnight is past, let us go to bed. We must rise early tomorrow to help Lady Harrington. Where does she get the energy from?"

The mixture being finished and put into tins and placed in the oven, they sat down at the table. "How long does the recipe say they take?" asked Jilly.

"Only fifteen minutes in a very hot oven," said Mandy, "and the oven is *very* hot. They are more like little biscuits than cakes."

"Then we will just have time to put our initials on them," said Jilly. "Oh, dear. It won't work anyway."

"Why not?"

"They are *dumb* cakes. We were supposed to bake them in silence. Now no one will come."

Mandy began to laugh. "I think we are become bewitched, believing in such stories. Who is going to call now?"

Lord Paul and Lord Ranger had left their friend Gully's home late and with reluctance. Had Gully not had a visitation from a large party of his relatives that evening who needed all the rooms, then both men would have stayed and forgotten the Tenbys.

They were riding down on horseback from Chipping Norton in the now thick, swirling snow. "Why didn't we take the carriage?" called Lord Ranger.

"Because we were frightened that Harriet and Lucinda might place themselves in it. Isn't Greenbanks around here?"

"You know very well that it is. Benham St. Anne's is to the left. Where are you going?"

"Demme, let's go to the Harringtons'. Use the snow as an excuse and be damned to Sir John!"

Sir John was coming back from the stables. The church bells were tolling the Old Lad's Passing Bell. The bell, which tolled the three days before Christmas from eleven until midnight, rang out for the death of the devil and the approaching birth of Christ.

And then Sir John stiffened and stood with his head on one side. He was sure he could hear the jingle of harness.

It was surely nearly midnight.

And then he heard the sound of horses, their hooves muffled by the snow. Lord Ranger and Lord Paul rode up to him and swung down from the saddle. "Our apologies, sir," said Lord Ranger, looking towards the darkened windows of the house. "I fear we have come too late."

"Never too late," said Sir John cheerfully. He suddenly saw a way he could make amends to his wife for having interfered in Jilly and Mandy's love life. "Tell you what. I see a light is still on in the kitchens. Jilly and Mandy are baking cakes. They put their initials on them, and the first person to arrive must put his initials beside theirs."

Lord Ranger looked towards the kitchens, which were on the ground floor to the side of the house in the old manner rather than in the basement. "Why?" he asked.

"Goodness knows," said Sir John easily. "Half the reasons for these old traditions have been lost in time. Off with you. No! I will attend to your horses. Used to it. Like horses. Oh, do go on!"

The door to the kitchens stood open.

"Thank goodness it is midnight," said Mandy. "I am so cold. When the bell finishes tolling, we can shut the door and go upstairs and get warm."

"There are voices in the yard," said Jilly. "Hush!"

"Someone is coming," said Mandy, turning quite pale. "Do you think . . . ?"

"No," said Jilly sharply. "Don't be ridiculous."

And then Lord Ranger and Lord Paul walked in through the open doorway.

"Where are these cakes?" asked Lord Ranger, swinging off his snow-covered cloak.

"M-Mine are here," said Jilly. "And Mandy's there."

Lord Ranger picked up a small vegetable knife from the kitchen table and solemnly pricked out his initials next to Jilly's, and Lord Paul put his next to Mandy's just as the church bell struck the last note.

"Now what happens?" asked Lord Ranger. "Do we turn into toads or something? I asked Sir John to explain the tradition, but he did not know."

So Sir John was the reason they had so miraculously appeared at the right moment.

Jilly flashed Mandy a little warning look. "We don't know either," she said. "Come upstairs. There is still some punch in the bowl to warm you."

Sir John was already in the drawing room, lighting a branch of candles. "Can't be bothered lighting those pesky lamps again," he said. "Punch, gentlemen?"

"Thank you," said Lord Ranger.

"Put your initials on the cakes, hey?" demanded Sir John.

"We did," said Lord Paul. "But the girls don't know the reason for the ritual either."

How do I handle this? thought Sir John. Do I tell them and scare them off? Leave it to the wife.

"You do Christmas in style, sir," said Lord Ranger, looking with appreciation round the room, at the decorations and the huge tree, at the presents piled on a table next to it, and at the Yule log, one end of which was in the fire and the other end out in the hall.

"But no mistletoe," said Lord Paul.

Sir John brightened. He knew his wife had warned everyone off kissing when there were only two berries left on the bough. He knew that she hoped that when the lords arrived—if they arrived—then those two last berries would be put to good use.

"We have a mistletoe bough over the entrance," said Sir John. "You came in at the wrong door."

"Then we must find some way of coming in at the right door tomorrow," teased Lord Ranger.

"Probably won't do much good," said Sir John slyly. "Only two berries left, and after the berries have gone, the kissing has to stop."

Lord Ranger looked at Jilly. She was wearing a plain gown covered with a green baize apron. There was a smudge of flour on her nose. He thought she looked enchanting.

"We must make use of them now," he said. "What do you say, Sir John?"

"A great idea," said Sir John. "And it will get rid of those berries. I had to kiss old Mrs. Chumley yesterday, and she was threatening to come back today to get another berry and another kiss."

Shyly Jilly and Mandy were escorted to the doorway.

Lord Ranger reached up and plucked one berry. He pulled Jilly close and the snow swirled around them. Then he bent and kissed her on the mouth. A jolt of raw passion went right through him. He forgot where he was, his mind as dizzy as the turning snow, his body on fire like the Yule log as his mouth sank deeper into the soft one beneath his own.

Mandy looked shyly up at Lord Paul, who was staring at his friend in surprise. He took down a berry and put it in his pocket. He gently kissed her on the lips. He was overcome with a feeling of protective tenderness such as he had never known before. He wanted to hold her so very close and keep the world away.

Sir John stood, shuffling from one foot to the other, wondering what to do.

Then he heard his wife's voice from the landing. "Why aren't those girl in their beds?"

The couples broke apart. Jilly reached out and took Mandy by the hand. "Good night," they both said shyly.

Both men stood in a sort of daze and watched them go.

Jilly and Mandy awoke early to the triumphant sound of the church bells. They dressed hurriedly, but neither of them talked about those kisses of the night before, as if to talk about the experience would diminish the glory of it.

Privately each hoped the miracle would go on, that in some way Lord Ranger and Lord Paul had decided to stay for Christmas day and not return to the Tenbys'. But then they could hear Lady Harrington calling for them and went down to the warmth of the kitchens to help with the final preparations for the enormous Christmas dinner, which was to be served at two in the afternoon.

Jilly and Mandy were preparing the vegetables to go with the turkey, and Lady Harrington was mixing a bowl of chestnut stuffing, when Sir John came into the kitchen with the two lords. Both girls immediately became conscious of their old dresses and that their hair had not been put up.

"No slackers or loungers here," said Lady Harrington. "All must help." Aprons were produced for the gentlemen, who complained that they were not supposed to do any work on Christmas day whatsoever.

Lord Ranger sat down at the kitchen table next to Jilly. Her face was flushed with the heat from the kitchen fire, and that glorious hair of hers cascaded down her back. Lord Paul sat next to Mandy, and both men were given bowls of potatoes to peel.

Then they were all ordered upstairs to dress for church. Jilly felt so elated, so breathless and excited, she thought she might cry. Off they went to church in pelisses trimmed with rich fur from one of Lady Harrington's old cloaks to sing carols and listen to the Christmas message.

As they walked back to Greenbanks after the service, Jilly with Lord Ranger and Mandy with Lord Paul, Jilly stopped suddenly and gave a little shiver.

"What is the matter?" asked Lord Ranger, looking curiously down at her.

"I felt suddenly cold," said Jilly, "as if something bad were about to happen."

"It is quite warm," he said, looking up at the bright sky. "Almost springlike and the snow is melting. Mrs. Tenby is going to be as cross as a bear, for the roads are clearing rapidly and we really have no excuse now to stay."

"But you will?"

He smiled down at her in a way that made her feel weak at the knees. "Yes, I will."

He tucked her arm in his and walked on. The bad moment had passed.

Jilly was never to forget that splendid Christmas dinner: the table groaning with food, Sir John at the end, benevolently carving the steaming turkey, Lady Harrington, now in her best gown and jewels, looking very grand as if she would not even know where her own kitchens were let alone go into them, and her own sharp awareness of Lord Ranger next to her.

The scholarly vicar, Mr. Crimmond, was telling the company—which included the curate, the schoolmaster, the squire and his family, and Mrs. Tibbs, the dressmaker, the Harringtons keeping a democratic table—the stories of Christmas, how the month of December coincided nicely with other, older festivals.

"Besides the Roman festivals already in existence," said Mr. Crimmond, "there was the Jewish Feast of Lights, Hanuca or Hanukkah, which went on for eight days in late December. This was a celebration of the strength of the Jewish faith, symbolized by the lighting of candles; one for the first night, two the next, and so on for eight days. This festival continues to this day," explained the vicar, "and games are played and presents exchanged. The idea of Christ as the light of the world was probably adapted by the church from this Jewish feast."

Then after the dinner, they all went through to the drawing room and opened their presents. The Harringtons had presents for everyone, even Lord Paul and Lord Ranger. They gave a great many presents during the year and received a great many, and so kept a box of them handy to give out to unexpected guests.

Jilly received a pearl necklace, and Mandy a coral one, Lady Harrington saying they were such plain little ornaments that their parents could not possibly take exception to the gifts.

Jimmy burst in, crying that Father Christmas

was coming, and all the candles on the Christmas tree were lit when Father Christmas, swinging his cudgel, walked ahead of the mummers into the room. He had a crown of holly on his head, his great red face was beaming with happiness and all he had already drunk, and his hooded red robe was opened to the waist. He was played by one of the local farmers. He walked round the room, reciting,

"Here comes I, old Father Christmas
Christmas comes but once a year
And when it comes it brings good cheer
Roast beef and plum pudding
And plenty of good old English beer.
Last Christmas time I turned the spit
I burnt my finger and can't find of it;
Then a spark fled over the table,
Saucepan got up and beat the ladle."

The nonsense rhyme went on, and then "King George" came in, played by the curate, transformed by cotton wool beard and paper crown, saying:

"I am King George, this notable knight,
I shed my blood for England's right.
England's right and England's glory all maintain."

He was followed by Bullslasher, the soldier, a character called Jack Finney, and the doctor, the doctor shouting, in reply to Father Christmas asking, "When doest thou come from?"

"Oh! All diseases!
Just what my box pleases.
Hard corns, soft corns,

Hipips, the phipps and palsy,
The gout and pains within
And pains all around about."

The nonsense went merrily on and finished with
the arrival of Helseybub, a black-looking devil covered in soot, who leered most dreadfully and pretended to attack the ladies, who fled from him,
shrieking with laughter.

As the mummers and Father Christmas were
helped to tankards from the wassail bowl, a carriage arrived and Mr. Travers, Mr. Jensen, Belinda
Charteris, and Margaret Andrews came in to join
them, Mr. Travers complaining loudly that all the
berries were gone from the mistletoe.

And no sooner had the mummers left than Lady
Harrington started to organize games. Christmas
games were a great tradition, the idea being to
make them as energetic as possible so that all the
food from the Christmas dinner would be shaken
down before the next banquet. They played Hunt
the Slipper, Forfeits, Blindman's Buff, Hide-and-
Seek, Port and Pair, Puss-in-the-Corner, and Row-
land Ho.

The Regency was a time of very strict formal
manners and conventions, but all those went to
the wall on Christmas day in homes other than the
Harringtons'.

There was a break while they all tucked into the
enormous mince pie. "What did you wish?" asked
Lord Ranger, watching Jilly take her first bite.

"I think I am not supposed to tell you," said Jilly,
but her wish had been loud and clear in her heart
and in her head: *If only you would marry me.*

After the mince pie was demolished along with

many other pies and sweets, they returned to the drawing room to play Snapdragon. Raisins, currants, and other dried fruit were heaped onto a shallow dish, brandy was poured on top of them, the lights were extinguished, and the brandy set on fire.

The idea was to snatch the fruit out of the flames, blow the flames out, and eat the fruit. While they all crowded around the flaming bowl, the squire sang the traditional song in a loud baritone:

> "Here he comes with the flaming bowl,
> Don't be mean to take his toll,
> Snip! Snap! Dragon!
>
> Take care you don't take too much,
> Be not greedy in your clutch,
> Snip! Snap! Dragon!"
>
> With his blue and lapping tongue
> Many of you will be stung,
> Snip! Snap! Dragon!"

Lord Ranger drew Jilly back from the bowl and into the darkness. He only knew he wanted to kiss her again and so he did, folding her tightly against him in the warm, brandy-scented, evergreen-scented room. He wanted to go on holding her and kissing her forever.

"Lights!" shouted Sir John, and they drew apart, staring up at each other in a dazed way as the lamps were lit again, and the candles on the tree.

"Did you bake dumb cakes?" Margaret asked.

Mandy nodded.

"And who came through the door at midnight?" asked Margaret.

"Lord Ranger and Lord Paul," said Mandy.

"Aha!" cried Belinda. "And did my lords put their initials next to those of our Davenport ladies?"

"Yes," said Lord Paul, "but no one seems to know the significance of that."

"I can tell you that," said Belinda with a gurgle of laughter and ignoring distressed and embarrassed looks from Jilly and Mandy. "Any lady who bakes a dumb cake and puts her initials on it knows that the gentleman who walks through the door at midnight and puts his initials next to her own is her future husband."

Jilly hung her head.

"You knew that, you wicked thing," said Lord Ranger, but his voice was full of affectionate laughter.

"Now charades," called Sir John.

Two maids carried in the hamper of costumes. They were all picking out cardboard crowns, tin swords, fake royal robes, and the door of the drawing room was propped open by the Yule log, when Lord Ranger suddenly saw Jilly's face turn paper white. She was staring at the doorway.

Everyone gradually followed her stricken gaze, saw the way she went to her sister and took her hand in her own.

The laughter died away. The room was silent except for the crackling of the fire.

Standing in the doorway, their faces masks of horror and with Abigail Biggs behind them, were Mr. and Mrs. Davenport.

Chapter Eight

"WHAT IS THE meaning of this idolatry?" demanded Mrs. Davenport, striding into the room. "And where did you get those disgraceful gowns?"

Jilly and Mandy were wearing two very pretty mulsin dresses.

Lady Harrington stood between the girls and their parents. "Merry Christmas," she said. "We were just enjoying Christmas day."

Mr. Davenport found his voice. "Paganism," he said awfully. "Paganism corrupting and soiling our daughters' virgin minds. I found them exposing themselves in disgraceful gowns and playing with *men*."

"No one's mind has been soiled," said Lady Harrington wrathfully, "unless it is your own. You have made your daughters' lives miserable with cruel treatment. Go away and leave them with me. I will care for them."

Mrs. Davenport walked round her and stood looking at Jilly and Mandy. "Take Abigail up to your rooms and get packed and be ready to leave. If you do not, you will force us to bring the magistrate to Lady Harrington. You are our daughters, and what we say, you must do. Go!"

Had Lord Ranger or Lord Paul said one word,

just one word, Jilly and Mandy might have tried to stand their ground. But what broke both their hearts was that both men were standing together, their faces an identical well-bred blank.

"We will wait in the carriage, Abigail," said Mrs. Davenport.

When Mr. and Mrs. Davenport had left the room and Jilly and Mandy had gone upstairs with Abigail, Margaret said, "What dreadful people. Can you not stop them, Lady Harrington?"

"I would if I could," she said sadly. "There is nothing to be done. I have no rights."

"What can *we* do?" asked Lord Ranger. "They cannot just leave like this."

Lady Harrington opened her mouth to snap at them that they could try proposing marriage but immediately realized that in the state of mind they were in, the Davenports would simply refuse to listen.

"Nothing, nothing," she said wearily. "Gather up their Christmas presents. They must not go without them."

She collected the presents and went upstairs with Sir John. The girls were in Jilly's bedroom, and there were discarded gowns lying on a pile on the bed.

"We shall not be taking these unsuitable garments with us, my lady," said Abigail with satisfaction.

"Don't be impertinent, you thing you, you creature, and know your place," said Lady Harrington, very stiffly on her stiffs. She called to her maids and ordered them to pack everything, including the presents.

Soon they were ready and the corded trunks were carried downstairs.

Lady Harrington held out her arms and hugged both girls. She whispered, "Try to stay unmarried until your majority, until you are both twenty-one, and then come to me. Your home is here."

Jilly and Mandy hugged her fiercely back.

Downstairs Lord Ranger took Jimmy aside and pressed a crown into his hand. "Be a good lad," he said, "and follow the Davenport coach. They may only go as far as Moreton and then rack up for the night. Return as fast as you can and tell me where they are. Don't tell anyone, mind."

Jimmy nodded, his eyes sparkling.

Lord Ranger, Lord Paul, and everyone crowded into the hall as the Davenport girls came downstairs. There were hugs and kisses all round and promises to write, and then Lord Ranger and Lord Paul, ignoring Abigail's baleful look, each kissed the girls on the cheek.

Jilly took one sad look through the open door of the drawing room, at the tree with its flickering candles, at the Yule log burning in the hearth, and at the decorations. Then taking Mandy's hand, she went out into the night.

The carriage bowled off. Mandy and Jilly sat like little statues as the crowd of people outside Greenbanks waved and cried out defiantly, "Happy Christmas. Godspeed!"

And then they were gone.

Somehow Christmas died with their going. Lady Harrington could do nothing but sob. Margaret and Belinda were crying as well. Sir John took Lady Harrington upstairs, and Mr. Travers and Mr. Jensen took Margaret and Belinda back to the Tenbys'.

Everyone else left until there was only Lord Ranger and Lord Paul, seated on either side of the fire.

"So, my silent friend," said Lord Paul, "does it not irk you to sit here inactive? We let them go, you know, without a word of protest, without giving those terrible Davenports a piece of our mind."

"All is not yet lost," said Lord Ranger. "I am waiting for something."

"What?" said Lord Paul sourly. "A miracle?"

"Listen!" He held up his hand and put his head on one side.

"For what? We have been here this age and I feel like bursting into tears like the ladies."

The door opened and Jimmy came in.

"Well?" demanded Lord Ranger.

"I followed them like you said, my lord. They are stopping at the White Hart in Moreton. I talked to the coachman, hired coach it is. They are going to Banbury on the morrow and on to Oxford if the weather holds good. From there they will catch the mail coach to the North."

"Good lad." Lord Ranger tossed him another crown, which Jimmy caught nimbly.

"So they're at the White Hart," said Lord Paul, after the boy had left. "So what are we supposed to do about it?"

"I am determined to have the little Jilly Davenport as my bride," said Lord Ranger. "Do you feel the same about t'other one?"

Lord Paul nodded. "But our suit will be refused, and out of sheer spite, too."

"So I think we should go adventuring again, my friend."

"What do you mean?"

"We will ride to the Tenbys' and collect our baggage and carriage. We will follow the Davenport coach when it leaves tomorrow, and as soon as we all find ourselves on a quiet stretch of the road, which should not be too difficult in midwinter, we will put on masks, hold up their coach, make off with the girls, and head for Gretna."

Lord Paul's black eyes lit up. "Capital. And that way we get our brides without having to put up with our in-laws."

Jilly and Mandy were in the same bedroom at the White Hart, the Davenports being unable to find them separate rooms during the busy Christmas season.

Despite the late hour, they sat in their private parlor at the inn and lectured their daughters on the sin and folly of their ways.

Both girls sat before them, heads hanging, lost in misery.

At last Mr. and Mrs. Davenport rose to their feet. "We will leave Abigail to put you both to bed, where you may reflect on the folly of your ways. And you will be chastised."

They both left the room and shut the door.

Abigail picked up a thin cane from behind one of the chairs where she had placed it and flexed it in her hands. "Now let's see if we can beat some sense into you," she said. "You first, Miss Mandy."

And then somehow all the memories of the glittering Christmas flew into Jilly's mind. She stood up and went to Abigail and wrenched the cane out of her hand.

"Get to your bed, woman," she said, "and leave us be. You weary us."

Abigail tried to seize the cane, but Jilly threw it contemptuously into a corner of the room.

The maid swung her hand to slap Jilly, but Jilly dodged and then gave the horrified Abigail a cracking slap across her beefy face.

Shocked out of her wits, Abigail began to scream and yell for help.

"Come, Mandy," said Jilly. She led her frightened sister out and along to their bedchamber, where she drew her inside and locked the door.

"That reign of terror is over," said Jilly calmly. "They will need to find another bully."

"Which they will," said Mandy through white lips.

The doorknob rattled and Mrs. Davenport's angry voice could be heard shouting, "Open this door," and then a chorus of voices came from the other rooms, telling her to keep quiet.

Jilly went up to the door and said, "We will see you in the morning, Ma. We are not going to open the door this night. You may do what you will with us when we reach home, but we will not be flogged by a servant in a public inn."

"Quite right," shouted a boozy voice from next door, and then Mrs. Davenport could be heard retreating.

"How can you be so brave?" marveled Mandy. "All hope went when he did not even react to their coming."

"Nor Lord Ranger either," said Jilly sadly, correctly interpreting the "he" to mean Lord Paul. "But in truth, what could either of them do?"

"Look sad. Look concerned. Show some emotion," said Mandy. "Not just stand there blankly as if witnessing some terrible social gaffe. I thought . . . I hoped . . . Oh, the feeling of loss is so hard to bear."

"We will need all our courage to deal with our parents," said Jilly. "We have had one marvelous holiday, which we will never forget, and two broken hearts, which will mend. And we have something to live for and fight for. Lady Harrington says we are to try to remain unmarried until our majority—you heard her, too. When that day arrives, when you, too, are twenty-one, then we will run away."

They undressed and washed and climbed into bed. "I am not brave at all," Mandy said, and began to cry. Jilly held her close. "We have each other. We must just hope and pray for courage."

Lucinda and Harriet listened and squirmed the next day as Mr. Travers told of how the Davenport girls had been ruthlessly taken away in the middle of the festivities. Adding to the misery was the news that both Lord Paul and Lord Ranger had left early in the morning without saying good-bye, only leaving Mrs. Tenby a rather curt note, thanking her for her hospitality. Instead of blaming themselves for the situation, they blamed Mrs. Tenby. It was all *her* fault for not having a more cheerful household and not being able to compete with the Harringtons. Christmas had been a rigidly formal if well-run affair.

Both had written to their parents to send for them as soon as possible. The fact that they had brought the contempt of the house party down on their well-coiffed heads themselves, they could not allow. Life was unfair and people were contrary and unkind. It served those Davenport girls right. They were better off in the wilds of Yorkshire. More their style. Anyone could see that.

Jilly and Mandy were finding themselves hard put to keep a brave face on it, facing their parents and Abigail over a breakfast in the private parlor. Abigail stood behind Mrs. Davenport's chair and her eyes held a sullen, foreboding look.

The wind had swung round to the east again, said the chatty waiter, and the short thaw was gone. Did madam notice the icicles? No one could ever remember having seen such big ones.

"We are not interested in your observations on the weather," said Mrs. Davenport, and her voice was so dripping with chill that the waiter swore afterwards that it was as if it dripped icicles like the eaves of the inn.

The silent breakfast over, they retired to their rooms to put on their outer garments. With one last brave show of defiance, Jilly and Mandy wore their altered gowns and the fur-lined pelisses. Jilly was wearing the pearl necklace, and Mandy, the coral one.

They climbed into the carriage. Jilly, looking out of the window, was remembering the dance, trying to remember every bright moment. The grim days had started all over again and they were going home.

The carriage jolted off, swung round at the front of the inn onto the Oxford road, and left Moreton-in-Marsh behind.

They climbed up the steep hills towards Chipping Norton, Mrs. Davenport averting her eyes from all the candles in the windows and all the evergreens that decorated the fronts of the houses.

Outside Chipping Norton they headed towards Banbury. The day was gray and quiet. They jolted along. The old rented carriage creaked like a square rigger in a chopping gale.

Would nothing happen to save them? wondered Jilly. Could not this antique carriage break a pole, snap a trace? But on they went, the afternoon growing quickly dark, her parents' faces opposite, two white blurs in the encroaching gloom.

Jilly was growing increasingly uneasy about Mandy. Her sister was so white, she looked as if she might faint at any moment. She herself had a hard lump of grief in her throat. She tried so very hard to think of the splendid fun she had had to console her, but all she could think about was Lord Ranger and being held in his arms in the warm darkness of the drawing room while the guests played Snapdragon.

But he had kissed her and said nothing of love and he had let her go without any show of sadness, without any protest.

A strong voice shouting something penetrated her thoughts. The carriage lurched to a halt.

The carriage door was wrenched open and a menacing masked figure holding a pistol ordered, "Out! All of you."

Abigail began to sob and scream. Jilly and Mandy climbed down and stood next to the coach, followed by their parents.

"We have nothing of value," said Mrs. Davenport.

"But you have," said the highwayman in a gruff, coarse voice. He pointed the pistol at Jilly and Mandy. "You two. Get in that carriage back there."

Jilly put her head back. "No, you will have to shoot us first."

"I won't shoot you," he sneered. "If you both don't do as you are told, I'll shoot your parents."

"Come, Mandy," said Jilly. She did not know why she was not afraid, only fired with an odd sort of blind courage.

"Forgive me," shouted Mrs. Davenport. "Don't go, my children. Take me instead. Oh, take me instead."

For a moment the tall highwayman seemed to be nonplussed, surprised. But he quickly rallied. "Who wants you?" he growled. "You two. Do as you are told."

Arms about each other's waists, Jilly and Mandy walked to the large traveling carriage that had stopped behind their coach. A muffled figure was on the box.

"And their baggage," ordered the highwayman, waving his pistol at the terrified coachman, who, babbling that he was a married man with five children, scrambled to get the trunks out of the rumble.

He was ordered to put them in the highwayman's carriage.

Jilly and Mandy opened the door of the other carriage and climbed inside. "We could open the far door," whispered Mandy, "and escape across the fields."

Her sister shook her head. "They would shoot us down."

They had not closed the door of the coach, however, in the hope they might find some way to escape, but the tall highwayman jumped inside and tapped on the roof, and the coach bowled off.

The highwayman removed his mask as the girls, huddled together, shrank back against the squabs.

"It is I, Ranger," he said.

Jilly stared at him, wide-eyed. "What are you about, my lord?"

"How could you terrify us like this?" cried Mandy.

"You are being abducted, ladies."

"Where are you taking us? To Lady Harrington's?"

She could not read his expression in the gloom, did not know that he was suddenly embarrassed. Usually very much in charge of every situation, Lord Ranger felt at a loss. What if he told them they were being taken to Gretna and they said they did not want to be married?

"Lord Paul is driving," he said instead. "We are taking you to a friend's outside Banbury. He is a friend from army days, Harry Simpson. We will explain all when we get there."

"But our parents, for all their faults, will be beside themselves with worry!" exclaimed Jilly.

"They will find a letter waiting for them at the posting house in Banbury," said Lord Ranger soothingly. "Lord Paul is keeping up a breakneck pace. We will soon be at the Simpsons'. Are you not happy to be rescued?"

"Oh, yes," said Jilly. But she took her sister's hand. She was very worried, her feelings in a turmoil. She had barely recovered from the fright of believing that Lord Ranger was a real highwayman. Now a new fear was taking hold of her mind. She had let him kiss her and caress her. He might have abducted her to make her his mistress!

She and Mandy sat in worried silence. Lord

Ranger could not bring himself to say anything about marriage, still worried that until they recovered from the shock of thinking they were being abducted by highwaymen, they would not be prepared to listen.

He looked out of the window and realized with relief that they were bowling up a long drive. It was a good thing that Harry Simpson was such an easygoing rattle, for they had not warned him of their impending arrival or that they were bringing two future brides with them.

Harry Simpson, an amiable man with a large nose and large feet, received Lord Paul and Lord Ranger in the hall with many cries of pleasure and welcome. Yes, he would be delighted to put them and their ladies up. Respectable ladies? Had to consider the wife's sensibilities.

Deadly respectable, said Lord Paul. Everything would be explained later. If they could just get the ladies indoors?

Mrs. Amy Simpson tripped down the staircase at that moment and hurled herself into Lord Ranger's arms. She was a dainty little blonde with a roguish eye, and Lord Ranger was suddenly reminded of the fact that Amy used to flirt with him and hoped she would not do so in front of Jilly.

Amy's blue eyes hardened a fraction when she was told about the waiting ladies, but she was intensely curious to find out what Lord Ranger was up to and so she said they must be brought in to the drawing room fire immediately.

She was relieved when Jilly and Mandy were led in by Lord Ranger. No one looking at such shivering waifs could ever imagine them to be other than respectable. For one awful moment Amy had feared that the two lords had brought their Cyprians.

"And where are you all going?" asked Amy brightly. "I see the ladies do not have a maid."

"Not now," said Lord Ranger. "We will explain later. Perhaps if the ladies could be shown to their rooms . . . ?"

"Of course," said Amy. "Our guests left last night and all the rooms have been cleaned and aired. Come with me."

She showed Jilly and Mandy upstairs and into adjoining bedchambers. "I will send my maid to help you change," said Amy. "Dinner is in an hour. We do not keep very fashionable hours in the country. Have you known Lord Ranger and Lord Paul long?"

"A few weeks," said Jilly nervously.

"Such a pair of rakes," said Amy lightly. "I always used to say to Ranger, 'No lady is safe with you.' That pair specialize in breaking hearts, I can assure you. But I gather I must not ask questions until this odd . . . er . . . affair is explained. Ring the bell if you require anything. Here are the maids to unpack your things."

The girls could not find an opportunity to talk about their fears because of the presence of the bustling servants. And no sooner had they left than a French lady's maid arrived to help them into their dinner gowns and to arrange their hair. She was a very sophisticated French lady's maid of a breed neither Jilly nor Mandy had met before, and she subtly made it obvious that she knew by looking at their dinner gowns that they had been made over, and by a provincial hand, too.

Then there was a footman in livery to lead them

downstairs to the drawing room, where they sat politely and listened as Harry rattled on about army days, and then in to dinner, where neither Jilly nor Mandy felt like eating much.

They answered questions about their Christmas with the Harringtons and then Amy rose as a sign that they were to follow her back to the drawing room and leave the gentlemen to their wine.

"Now," said Harry, "what's this all about? Not like you to cavort around the countryside with a couple of scared virgins, hey?'"

"We abducted them," said Lord Ranger, "on the Banbury road. We snatched them from their parents."

Harry dropped his wineglass and it shattered on the table.

"You *what*? Look, I want no part in this."

"You do not understand," Lord Ranger said, and patiently began to tell Harry the whole story and about the planned flight to Gretna.

Harry stared at them in amazement. "That puts a different light on the matter now that I know your intentions are at least honorable. But there are two very scared ladies there. Are you sure they want to marry you?"

"We haven't asked them yet," said Lord Paul.

"Here's a coil. Mayhap they think you have taken them away for other purposes."

"How could they think that?"

"Because," said Harry patiently, "at no point in your story did I hear anything about declarations of undying love. You'd best get through to the drawing room and get to it or you'll have that pair running off into the night, thinking they are saving themselves from a fate worse than death."

Amy was telling the girls another story about the exploits of Lord Paul and Lord Ranger. "There were these two Spanish señoritas in Madrid," she was saying, "who were enamored of that pair, and their parents called on our lords and threatened to shoot them if they did not back off. What heartbreakers." Amy twisted a golden curl in her fingers and looked slyly at Jilly. "That terrible rogue, Ranger, set out to break my heart as well. And me, a married woman!" She looked up as the door opened and the men walked in.

"Come along, my dear," said her husband. "They need to talk. Paul, you can take Miss Mandy to the Green Saloon, and we will leave Ranger here with Miss Jilly."

Jilly reached out to stop her sister leaving, but Mandy was looking up into Lord Paul's eyes as he led her out and seemed suddenly oblivious to everything else.

When they were both left alone, Lord Ranger held out his hand. "Come here to me, Jilly."

She backed away and said in a trembling voice, "There are no parents here, my lord, nor Lady Harrington either. I must ask you your intentions."

He crossed the room to where she stood in front of the fireplace and went down on one knee in front of her.

"Miss Davenport," he said solemnly, "will you marry me?"

"Why?" asked Jilly.

He stood up and drew her into his arms. "Because I love you with all my heart. We are going to be married at Gretna, and then if your parents ever forgive us, we will be properly married in church on our return from the North. Kiss me, Jilly, for heaven's sake, girl, and tell me I have not made the most disastrous mistake."

Her eyes were suddenly full of tenderness and laughter. "I love you with all my heart, and yes, I will marry you. I cannot believe the nightmare is over."

He kissed the tip of her nose, then her cheeks and then her mouth, and he was kissing her with increasing intensity when the door opened and Mandy and Lord Paul walked in hand in hand to join them.

Mr. and Mrs. Davenport were sitting in their private parlor in the Spread Eagle at Banbury, waiting for the arrival of the magistrate and the head of the local militia.

"It is a judgment on us," said Mrs. Davenport tearfully. "My precious girls. My babies. We were too harsh on them. It's all your fault, Abigail. You *enjoyed* tormenting them."

There was a scratching at the door, which then opened to reveal Peter, the footman, from Colonel Tenby's. He bowed low and held out a letter. "Mr. and Mrs. Davenport, this is for you."

Mrs. Davenport took the letter and broke open the seal. It was a long letter from Lord Ranger, and she read it several times as if unable to believe her eyes. In it he said that he and Lord Paul had pretended to be highwaymen. They were taking Jilly and Mandy to Gretna to marry them over the anvil at the blacksmith's. If the Davenports hounded them or tried to bring them back, then both he and Lord Paul would be happy to expose in court all the misery that the Davenports had inflicted on their daughters. On the other hand, they could accept the marriage with good grace and so avoid scandal.

He apologized for all the distress he had caused them but assured them he was convinced that it was nothing compared to the distress such unnatural parents had caused their own children. He begged to remind the Davenports that he and Lord Paul were the sons of dukes and not without power.

At last she looked up, her eyes blank with shock, and said to the waiting Peter, "You may go. There is no reply." Then she handed the letter to her husband.

After he read it, he said wrathfully, "Will that magistrate never arrive? I will have them hunted down and those girls dragged back. I will—"

"No!" said Mrs. Davenport in a trembling voice. "Do you not see how it will make us look? We will be in the newspapers. We will be vilified. We should never have left Yorkshire."

"But they are our daughters," cried Mr. Davenport. "We cannot let this happen."

"It has happened," said his wife. She straightened her gown and stiffened her spine. "The devil has entered the souls of our girls. It is not our fault. Nothing we have done has caused this."

And so they consoled each other until the magistrate arrived to hear with surprise that Mrs. Davenport had had a "queer" turn and had imagined everything.

Chapter Nine

*L*ADY HARRINGTON was glad the long winter and chilly spring had ended at last, bringing blue skies back to the Cotswolds. The hedgerows were heavy with Queen Anne's lace and hawthorn blossom and the delicate fresh green of young leaves that had not yet acquired the dull green of midsummer.

She often thought of Jilly and Mandy. She had lost two baby daughters in a smallpox epidemic many years ago, and the Davenport girls were what she had dreamed her own girls would grow up to be. She imagined Jilly and Mandy being crushed and berated and beaten until there was nothing left of their happiness and warmth and affection.

Many times Sir John had had to stop her from setting out to the North. There was nothing they could do, he kept saying. The Davenport girls had left their mark on the village. The vicar, the schoolmaster, and the curate constantly called to ask if there was any news. Margaret Andrews had written from London with the glad news that she was engaged to be married to Mr. Travers and that Belinda Charteris was engaged to Mr. Jensen and had also asked if anything had been heard.

Even Colonel Tenby had called on a brief leave, saying that the visit of the Davenport girls had changed his life, for his wife was now more pleasant in every way and had even confessed to bribing Mr. Nash and had got his precious plate back.

Lady Harrington, in an effort to try to find out if Lord Ranger or Lord Paul had shown any remorse at having let the girls go so easily, had written to friends in London asking about their whereabouts, but no one had seen them. The Season had started, Lucinda and Lady Harriet were to be seen everywhere, but there was no sign of either lord.

She often went for a walk by the pond, looking out at the sunny waters, imagining it covered once more with ice, seeing Jilly and Mandy spinning about on their skates, laughing and carefree.

She was standing one day as usual by the pond. A lilac tree sent purple blossoms onto the surface of the water, blown by a light warm wind. As usual, she was thinking of Jilly and Mandy, hoping they were well, trying to banish black images of them being forced to marry unsuitable men. She hoped that Sir John had been right, and that the bright memories they had given them might help them to be brave.

And then she heard the sound of a carriage out on the road and looked towards the open gates at the end of the short drive, wondering if the squire had come to call.

A very grand coach indeed turned in at the gates, driven by a splendid coachman in a white wig seated on a gold hammercloth-covered box.

She turned and hurried up to the house to greet these unexpected visitors.

Two ladies and two gentlemen were alighting. She stopped still and then held her arms wide. Jilly and Mandy, dressed in the very height of fashion, threw themselves into her arms, laughing and crying as Sir John came out to see what was causing all the noise.

At last Lady Harrington drew back and looked at their rich clothes and then towards where Lord Ranger and Lord Paul were standing, and her face hardened.

"What has happened here?" she demanded. "I read of no wedding announcements."

"We *are* married," said Jilly. "We will tell you all about it."

"Married!" Now Lady Harrington began to cry in earnest, saying between sobs that she had been so worried about them, had imagined them being starved and beaten and locked in dark cupboards, until Sir John said cheerfully that they would all be more comfortable indoors.

Jilly looked about the drawing room that she had once thought never to see again. There were bowls of flowers all about the room and a lazy little fire smoked in the hearth, nothing like the gigantic bonfire caused by that Christmas Yule log.

Lord Ranger settled down beside her on the sofa and took her hand, staring for a moment at his wife in delight as if not yet quite used to the fact she was really his.

Lady Harrington dried her eyes and listened eagerly to the tale of masquerading as highwaymen, of the long journey to Gretna, then of the journey south, Lord Ranger taking Jilly to meet his parents, and Lord Paul bearing off Mandy to introduce her to his. Then they had come together once more because the girls had a request, that they stay with Lady Harrington and be married in the village church of Benham St. Anne's.

"And so you shall!" cried Lady Harrington. "But why did you not put a notice in the newpapers?"

"There will be one in today," said Lord Ranger, "announcing our forthcoming marriages. To state that we were married already, and at Gretna, would have caused a great deal of unnecessary scandal."

"So what of your parents?" asked Lady Harrington. "Have they forgiven you?"

"We wrote to them to say we were coming here to stay," said Jilly, "and that if they wished to see us properly married in church, they were welcome to come. I hope we have not presumed too much, my lady. But we did so want to surprise you."

"We will give you a wedding to remember," said Lady Harrington. "But wedding gowns! You do not want provincial wedding gowns."

"We have splendid wedding gowns in our baggage," said Mandy. "Lord Paul's mother, the Duchess of Barshire, insisted on ordering them for us. We shall be so grand. Oh, it is so good to be home."

"Yes, it is home to us," said Jilly.

"And where will you live?" asked Sir John.

"We shall settle somewhere near here," said Lord Ranger. "Jilly wants somewhere exactly like Greenbanks."

"You will find it easy to find a place," remarked Sir John. "So many families are ruined at the gambling tables of St. James's and have to put their estates on the market."

"Come, girls," said Lady Harrington, getting to her feet. "You shall have your old rooms."

Sir John gave a little cough. "Not their old rooms *exactly*, my dear. Married ladies now."

"Goodness, my wits are wandering. Jilly's old

room is quite suitable for herself and her husband, and Mandy's old room can be used by both of them as a dressing room, and Mandy and Lord Paul can have the Blue Room, which James uses when he is here."

Laughing and chattering, they went up the old staircase, Jilly saying over and over that they had never expected to see Greenbanks again.

The cheerful maids bustled about, unpacking their clothes. Jimmy was sent off to the village to carry the glad news, and soon a little procession, headed by the squire, Sir William Black, and his family, could be seen heading up the drive.

Will I ever be as competent as Lady Harrington? thought Jilly as that lady calmly coped with this unexpected houseful of guests and visitors.

Mr. and Mrs. Davenport were returning from a visit to neighbors. There was no Abigail with them. They had pensioned her off, persuading each other that the reason was that their girls had left so there was no further need for her services, where the real reason was that the very sight of her filled them with guilt. They were convinced Jilly and Mandy were living in sin with a couple of aristocratic rakes who had seduced them. They had given up scanning the newspapers, hoping for some kind of announcement.

Mrs. Davenport had written many angry letters to the Harringtons, accusing them of having corrupted their daughters, but somehow had not the heart to post any of them.

Pride had forced them to tell their friends and neighbors that their daughters were still in the South on an extended visit. They were so used to being smugly righteous that they hardly knew how to cope with all these new feelings of nagging guilt. Their attendance at church had slowly fallen off. Once they had gone every day of the week. Now they only went reluctantly on Sundays. There was a new vicar, not like the old hellfire one, who preached love and charity, and sometimes the miserable Davenports felt he had guessed their secret and was speaking directly to them.

The postboy sounded his horn outside, but Mrs. Davenport remained where she was. For the past few months, she had run out to meet him, hoping for news until hope had died.

The footman came in and bent low before Mrs. Davenport with a silver tray on which several letters lay. In practically every other household, the post was given to the master, but Mrs. Davenport had made it clear long ago that she expected to read all letters first.

She took the letters and opened the first one, which was sealed with a heavy blob of wax embossed with a crest.

She stared down at the first lines and then looked at the signature at the bottom of the page. "It is from Jilly," she said weakly. "I cannot read it."

Her husband twitched it out of her hands, scrabbled in the folds of his cravat for his quizzing glass, and then studied it.

"Jilly is married," he said in a wondering voice, "to Lord Ranger, and Mandy to Lord Paul. They were married at Gretna, but both want to be remarried in church. They have gone to Lady Harrington's to be married there and say that if we join them, we are more than welcome!"

He took the other letters. There was one from

Mandy, one from Lord Ranger, and one from Lord Paul.

"Lord Paul says the notice of the forthcoming marriage has been sent to the newspapers and that both his parents and Lord Paul's will be in attendance."

Mrs. Davenport had begun to cry. She felt as if the weight of centuries had been lifted from her.

"Of course, we would not dream of attending," said Mr. Davenport wrathfully. "To have connived in that highwaymen masquerade, to have shamed our name, to have gone to those Harringtons, who caused all the trouble in the first place . . ."

But his wife was not listening. She rubbed her eyes and then said in a firm voice, "I have heard Lord Paul's mother, the Duchess of Barshire, is vastly fashionable. There is no time surely to have something made, but I had my purple gown made in London. Yes, that will do very well. Oh, so much to arrange. Oh, thank God!"

And leaving her amazed husband staring after her, she bustled from the room.

Lady Harrington was walking with Jilly by the pond the day before the wedding. "You must not let the absence of your mother and father upset you, dear," she said. "They do not deserve your concern."

"They *are*, however, our mother and father," said Jilly in a low voice, "and somehow I would have liked their blessing. They were, you see, both of them brought up very strictly and they continued with us. I can see now that I am removed from them that they were doing what they thought best for us."

"Well, *I* hope they don't come. I have enough on my hands," snapped Lady Harrington, who was feeling the strain of having two dukes and two duchesses who expected strict formality under her roof.

Both had arrived with retinues of servants who had to be billeted in and around the village, and both had insisted that their footmen be present to serve all meals and that their French chefs take control of the kitchens. Lady Harrington sighed. Having such an abundance of servants should have made life easier, but there were just too many of them, and the footmen had to be watched every moment in case they seduced the Harrington maids.

"I am glad to hear your in-laws are leaving directly after the wedding," said Lady Harrington. "I feel like one of those poor landowners surviving a visit from Queen Elizabeth."

Marquees were being erected in the gardens to house the guests. Colonel Tenby had arrived home for the wedding and had insisted on housing as many of the guests as he could.

They walked back together side by side to the house.

Then Jilly looked down the drive and said in an amazed voice, "But that is *our* carriage."

"So? What of it? Probably Lord Ranger and Lord Paul coming back from somewhere."

"No," said Jilly. "I mean my parents' carriage. They have come."

As they reached the house, Mandy came out with Lord Ranger and Lord Paul.

Jilly and Lady Harrington joined them. "Remember," urged Lady Harrington, "they can do nothing to you now."

The steps were let down and the Davenports descended.

Mrs. Davenport, dressed more fashionably than either of her daughters had ever seen her, stood looking at them for a moment and then said in a small voice they had never heard her use before, "We are come for your wedding."

Jilly and Mandy ran to hug her, and Mrs. Davenport began to cry while Mr. Davenport furiously blew his nose.

Lady Harrington drew Lord Ranger and Lord Paul into the house. "Leave them to it," she said crossly. "Though, by God, it's more than that precious pair deserve."

The little church was crowded the next day and the streets leading to the village were jammed with carts, gigs, and post chaises, everyone having traveled from far and wide to see this fashionable double wedding.

Margaret Andrews and Belinda Charteris had traveled from London to be bridesmaids. Lady Harrington clutched her husband's hand hard as Mr. Davenport, with a daughter on each arm, walked up the aisle.

The girls were in white Brussels lace embroidered with rich gold thread and seed pearls. Each had a coronet of pearls and gold wire holding their veils.

Lady Harrington's eyes filled with tears and she dabbed them furiously with her handkerchief. On her other side Mrs. Davenport began to weep as well.

For both of them the service passed in a tear-soaked blur until the village band broke into a jolly tune and the bells in the steeple crashed out to proclaim the glad tidings to the waiting crowd outside that Jilly and Mandy were married.

Somehow drawn together now, Lady Harrington and Mrs. Davenport stood together as Jilly and Mandy were helped into the flower-bedecked wedding carriage and were then followed by their husbands. Flower petals were thrown from all around. The crowd sent up a great cheer and the carriage moved off through the crowded narrow village street.

Everyone vowed the wedding was the best ever once the marquees were full to bursting point with everyone eating and drinking, for Lady Harrington had invited the whole village.

Then there was dancing and then suddenly Lord Ranger and Lord Paul escorted their brides from the marquee and went towards the house.

"Thank goodness it all went so well," said Lady Harrington to Mrs. Davenport. "Tomorrow when they have all gone, you and I will put our feet up and have a comfortable coze."

"It is a wonder they don't hate me," mumbled Mrs. Davenport.

"What *you* need," said Lady Harrington firmly, "is a glass of champagne."

"I never drink!"

"It is your daughters' wedding. Have one glass and we will toast them."

Soon Mrs. Davenport was sipping champagne. Her husband looked about to protest, but then he changed his mind. In his mind's eye he still walked down that aisle with two of the most beautiful girls in the world.

Lord Ranger slowly undid the tapes at the back of his wife's wedding dress and let it fall to the floor.

"What are you thinking about?" he asked softly, turning her around to face him.

"I was thinking about Christmas," said Jilly. "I was thinking that miracles do happen."

He picked her up in his arms and carried her to the bed and removed the rest of her clothes and then his own. No one, he thought with a burst of gladness as he gathered that well-loved body into his arms, had ever told his unsophisticated bride that ladies should not indulge in passion.

And then as he covered her naked body with his own and began to kiss her, he forgot about everything else.